A Change of Heart

A Change of Heart

A HARMONY NOVEL

Philip Gulley

HarperSanFrancisco

A Division of HarperCollins*Publishers*

In addition to writing, Philip Gulley also enjoys the ministry of speaking. If you would like more information, please contact:

David Leonards
3612 North Washington Boulevard
Indianapolis, IN 46205–3592
317–926–7566
ieb@prodigy.net

If you would like to correspond directly with Philip Gulley, please send mail to:

Philip Gulley
c/o HarperSanFrancisco
353 Sacramento St.
Suite 500
San Francisco, CA 94111

HarperCollins books may be purchased for educational, business, or sales promotional use. For information please write: Special Markets Department, HarperCollins Publishers, Inc., 10 East 53rd Street, New York, NY 10022.

HarperCollins Web site: http://www.harpercollins.com
HarperCollins®, ♣®, and HarperSanFrancisco™ are
trademarks of HarperCollins Publishers, Inc.

FIRST HARPERCOLLINS PAPERBACK EDITION PUBLISHED IN 2006

Library of Congress Cataloging-in-Publication Data
Gulley, Philip.
A change of heart : a Harmony novel / Philip Gulley. — 1st ed.
p. cm.
ISBN-13: 978–0–06–083455–5
ISBN-10: 0–06–083455–2
1. Harmony (Ind.:Imaginary place)—Fiction. 2. City and town life—Fiction.
3. Indiana—Fiction. 4. Quakers—Fiction. 5. Clergy—Fiction. I. Title
PS3557.U449C465   2005
813'.54—dc22   2005040319

06 07 08 09 10 RRD(H) 10 9 8 7 6 5 4 3 2 1

To Lyman and Harriet Combs,
who changed my heart

CONTENTS

One

A Monument to Romance

*I*t was the Tuesday after Easter, and Sam and Barbara Gardner were reclining underneath a palm tree, their eyes closed, their bodies ghostlike after a long winter.

"This is the life," Sam said, sipping his ginger ale, then sighing contentedly.

"It's not quite what I had in mind," Barbara said.

"What do you mean, it isn't what you had in mind?"

"When I agreed to be in charge of the church's Easter program in exchange for your taking me somewhere with palm trees, I wasn't thinking of the Holidome in Cartersburg."

"You should have been more specific," Sam pointed out.

"We could have at least spent the night."

"Are you crazy? They want eighty dollars a night."

"And you're sure we won't get in trouble for using the pool?"

"Not so long as they don't catch us," Sam said. "Just act like you belong."

Barbara sighed. "Steve Newman is a podiatrist and has a vacation condominium in Florida."

"Who's Steve Newman?"

"A guy I dated in college, before I met you. He wanted to marry me, but I turned him down. Now he owns a chain of podiatry offices in Ohio and spends the winter in Florida."

"Why didn't you marry him?"

"He gave me the creeps. He kept wanting to touch my feet."

Sam gazed at her feet. "I can't fault him. You have lovely feet."

"You think so?" She lifted her feet to inspect them.

"I especially like your thin ankles."

"Oh, Sam, you always know just what to say."

"It's a minister thing. Seventeen years of being diplomatic."

Barbara reclined her lounge chair until it was flat, then turned to lie on her stomach.

"Would you like me to rub suntan lotion on your back?" Sam offered.

"In case you haven't noticed, we're inside."

"We can pretend, can't we?"

"In that case, sure."

Sam squirted out a gob of lotion in his hand and began rubbing Barbara's back.

"Be careful not to get any on my feet," she cautioned. "I don't want the sand to stick to me."

"Now you're catching on."

They sat by the pool another hour, then rose and made their way to a table to eat lunch. Baloney sandwiches with ketchup, which Sam had made at home, along with potato chips and HoHos. Sam went to the vending machine and bought them a Coke to share.

They lasted another hour before the manager invited them to leave.

"I believe that was a record," Barbara said on the drive home.

"What record is that?"

"The cheapest date ever."

"I thought it was creative," Sam said, slightly hurt.

"Dr. Pierce is taking Deena scuba diving in Belize for their honeymoon. That's creative."

"I thought you liked our honeymoon."

"Sam, you know I liked it. Cincinnati was nice." She reached over and took his hand. "I just thought when you said you'd take me somewhere with palm trees, you didn't mean Cartersburg. Those weren't even real palm trees."

"Speaking of Dr. Pierce and Deena," Sam said, eager to change the subject, "I had a good premarital counseling session with them. Did you know his great-grandfather was the Pierce in Pierce-Arrow?"

"Who's Pierce-Arrow?"

"Pierce-Arrow is a what, not a who. They made cars. That's where Dr. Pierce got his money."

"I didn't know he had money."

"Quite a handsome amount, according to Deena. I hope he tithes," Sam said wistfully. "We could use some new hymnals."

"That's going to take a lot more than money. That's going to take Bea and Opal Majors dying."

"I can dream, can't I?"

"Sam Gardner, for a minister you sure are cynical."

Some days, cynicism was all that got Sam through.

It was his fifth year of ministry at Harmony Friends Meeting, which was about four years and eleven months longer than he'd predicted when he'd agreed to become their pastor. To be honest, Sam wasn't sure whether to attribute his tenure to the Holy Spirit or insanity. He'd once read that insanity was doing the same thing over and over, but expecting a different result. This described his five years to a tee. Each Sunday he preached about becoming a new creation, each week his congregation refused to become it, and the next Sunday found Sam preaching about it again.

On a more positive note, Harmony Friends Meeting was finally beginning to grow, Dale Hinshaw was hinting he might join the Baptist church, and the thirty-year-old spinster Deena Morrison had snagged herself a man.

They crested the hill in front of Ellis and Miriam Hodge's

farm and spied the town's water tower on the horizon. It was built in the summer of 1929 by a metalworks company from the city. When the tower was finished, the town closed Main Street and threw a party for the workers, one of whom waltzed with a beautiful, young lady; they fell in love and two months later were married.

He quit his job at the metalworks company, opened a welding shop, and bought a house on Poplar Street, at the base of the water tower. They had the best water pressure in town. He could shower in the basement while she washed dishes and never miss a lick. Seven years into their marriage they had a daughter named Gloria, who later gave birth to a boy named Samuel. As far as Sam knows, his grandparents were the first couple ever brought together by public utilities. He thinks about them whenever he sees the water tower rising above the town, a monument to romance.

"Have I ever told you how my grandparents met?" Sam asked Barbara.

About a million times, she thought. Desperate to change the subject, she pointed to a mobile home sitting in a field. "I wonder who lives there?" she asked.

"Oh, that. That's where Ellis Hodge's brother, Ralph, lived with his wife. Remember, they moved here with Amanda, and Ellis bought them that trailer. Then they went off to California and left Amanda with Ellis and Miriam." Sam paused. "Drinkers."

"Ellis and Miriam are drinkers?"

"No, Ralph and his wife. That's how Ellis and Miriam ended up with Amanda."

She'd heard that story a million times too, but it was a shorter story.

"Anyway," Sam continued, determined to finish his family's tale, "my mother's father came here in 1929. I think it was in May, but it might have been June. Anyway, he came here to build the water tower and when it was done—"

"He met your grandma and they were married and had great water pressure and your mom was born and met your dad, then you were born. Yes, I've heard that story."

"Boy, you're not just kidding about that water pressure," Sam said. "It'd peel your hide right off." He sighed. "I wish we had water pressure like that."

"Well, honey, we can't have everything."

"I suppose you're right," Sam admitted, sounding rather woeful.

They passed the old tourist cabins, built before the interstate, when Harmony was on the road to the city. The cabins now rent by the week, mostly to single men down on their luck. Two blocks later, out front of the Dairy Queen, Oscar Purdy was perched on a ladder putting letters on the sign.

"*NOW HIRI*," Sam read. "I wonder what *NOW HIRI* is. It sounds Japanese."

"It's *NOW HIRING*," Barbara said, as Oscar slid an *N* into place. "For crying out loud, Sam, he puts the same sign up every year. You think you'd know that by now."

"I was just kidding."

Bob Miles, the editor of the *Harmony Herald,* was peering out his office window.

"Duck," Sam commanded.

Barbara slid down in her seat. "Why am I ducking?"

"It's Tuesday. He's writing his 'Bobservation Post' column. If he sees us together, he'll write about it and everyone will ask me what we were doing when I was supposed to be at the church today."

She slid down farther.

"Rats."

"What's wrong?" Barbara asked.

"The light turned red. Stay down. He's looking right at us."

Three weeks earlier a state highway truck had rolled into town and they installed a traffic light at the corner of Main and Washington, in front of the *Herald* building and Kivett's Five and Dime. Bob Miles had editorialized against the unbridled power of state government. Before the stoplight had been installed, he could count on a car wreck each week to plump up the front page of the *Herald*. There hadn't been a wreck since, newspaper readership was down 25 percent, Bob was desperate for hard news, and everyone in town was trying their utmost not to become it.

Sam turned left at the light and headed toward home. There was a small knot of people gathered outside Grant's Hardware.

Sam slowed to a stop. Asa and Jessie Peacock were standing at the edge of the crowd, looking anxious.

Sam leaned out the window. "What's going on?"

Asa and Jessie hurried over to Sam's car. "It's Dale Hinshaw. Something's awful wrong with him," Asa said. "We called Johnny Mackey to come with his ambulance, but he's not here yet."

It would stagger the mind to know how many people in our town have died in the past thirty years waiting for Johnny Mackey to arrive with his ambulance.

Sam jumped from the car and ran to Dale, edging people aside. Dale was stretched out on the pavement. His shirt was loosened around his neck and his feet were propped up. He was deathly pale.

"Hey, Dale," Sam said, bending down beside him.

Dale's eyes fluttered open. His lips moved, but no sound came out. The one time Sam wanted Dale to speak, and he wouldn't.

"What happened?" Sam asked urgently, looking around the crowd of people. "Who knows what happened?"

"He was coming out of Grant's and he just sorta fell over," Bea Majors said. "I saw the whole thing. I was sitting in the chair at the Kut 'n' Kurl getting my hair fixed. Do you like it?"

Dale groaned.

"What is it, Dale?" Sam asked, leaning over to place his ear near Dale's mouth.

"I'm . . . going . . ." Dale said weakly, then fell silent.

"He's in no shape to go anywhere, if you ask me," Bea said.

"I think he stopped breathing," Uly Grant said.

"Does anyone know CPR?" Jessie Peacock asked, glancing around anxiously.

To his credit, Sam Gardner didn't even consider how much easier his life would be with Dale gone. He dropped to his knees, tilted Dale's head back, pinched off his nose, placed his mouth squarely on Dale's, and exhaled mightily.

Back and forth he moved, compressing Dale's chest, then blowing in his mouth. Five minutes passed, then ten. Johnny Mackey was nowhere in sight, a larger crowd had gathered, and Sam was tiring.

"Let me help," Deena Morrison said, stepping forward from the cluster of people. "You compress, and I'll breathe."

Several of the men in the crowd considered collapsing to the sidewalk themselves so Deena would press her lips to theirs.

It took Johnny Mackey twenty minutes to arrive with his ambulance. "Had to get gas," he explained.

Meanwhile, Jessie Peacock had gone to fetch Dr. Neely, who arrived just as Johnny pulled up. By then, Dale appeared to be rallying. His color was returning, and his breathing had evened out. Sam and Asa lifted him onto the gurney and loaded him in the ambulance. Dr. Neely climbed in after Dale, Johnny switched the siren on, and off they drove toward the hospital in Cartersburg.

Sam sat on the curb, exhausted, his body aching with spent adrenaline.

"You saved his life, Sam," Asa said.

Sam couldn't tell whether Asa was pleased with him or not.

"What's going on here?" asked Bob Miles, pushing his way into the center of the crowd.

"Sam and Deena just saved Dale's life," Jessie Peacock said. "They gave him CPR."

Bob was thoroughly disgusted. "And I missed it! Why didn't someone come get me? I could have put a picture of it on the front page."

Kyle Weathers, the town barber and perpetual bachelor, spoke up. "We could do a photo re-creation like they do on those cop shows on television. I'll lie down and Deena can give me mouth-to-mouth." He eased himself down to the sidewalk and looked up expectantly at Deena.

"Not in your wildest dreams," she said.

"Come on, honey, let's get going to the hospital to be with the Hinshaws," Barbara said to Sam, taking him by the arm and guiding him toward their car.

"Just think," Sam said, after a few steps. "If we had gone where they had real palm trees, I wouldn't have been here to save Dale's life."

"Yes, I guess you're right," she said, leaning her head into him and squeezing his hand. "I'm awfully proud of you."

Sam beamed, secretly hoping the day wouldn't come when he would regret what he had done.

Two

Opening Day

T wo weeks passed, it was mid-April, and the crocuses around Fern Hampton's mailbox were in bloom. Oscar Purdy had hired a small army of high-school girls to work the counter and was contemplating opening the Dairy Queen early in light of the warm weather that had graced the town.

Uly Grant had ordered in his summer supply of lawn mowers and arrayed them on the sidewalk across the front of the hardware store, drawing old men out of doors to inspect this year's models.

"Would you look at that," Stanley Farlow said, nudging a mower with the toe of his boot. "Nothing but plastic. I wouldn't give you twenty dollars for the whole lot of 'em. And Hondas to

boot. I tell you one thing, if Uly'd had those little nippers shoot-
ing at him in the Big War, he wouldn't be selling their mowers.
I'll tell you that right now."

"I got a Honda and it's been a good mower," Harvey
Muldock ventured.

Few subjects are able to generate contention among old men
like lawn mowers, lawn mowing being a religion in Harmony.
Each man is a devotee of his particular brand and will argue to
the death for its superiority, as if picking the right lawn mower
confirms his worth as a human being.

"If you ask me, John Deere's the way to go," Asa Peacock said.

Stanley Farlow snorted. "You're just paying for the green
paint. Now, you take Snapper. I've been using the same Snapper
for twenty years now, and it does just fine. Doesn't burn a drop
of oil and has a nice, even cut."

"What are you talking about?" Harvey asked. "That yard of
yours looks pitiful. I thought maybe you'd been cutting your
grass with a dull ax. I'm glad you told me it was a Snapper. Now
I know not to buy one."

They stood in front of the hardware store another half hour,
circling like bulldogs nipping at one another's heels, until Uly
came out and shooed them along.

Uly has been thinking of getting a restraining order against
Stanley Farlow. Potential customers walking past slow down to
view the mowers, which is Stanley's cue to enlighten them. "You
don't want that mower. Nothin' but junk. I tell you, it's highway

robbery what he's askin' for these mowers. He oughta be ashamed of himself. You buy that mower and you're buying yourself a peck of trouble."

Sam walked past several times, waiting for Stanley to leave, so he could look at the mowers without having to endure editorial comment. Sam had inherited his grandfather's mower, which was held together with duct tape and baling wire. He'd used it for five years before pronouncing it dead and hauling it to the dump, over the objections of his father, who believed the mower was good for another ten years at least.

His father drove to the dump, retrieved it, and stored it in his garage along with all the other "perfectly good things that just need a little elbow grease and they'll be as good as new." Sam's father has nine perfectly good mowers in his garage awaiting resurrection.

After a bit of haggling for a 10 percent clergy discount and a free tank of gas, Sam settled on a mower. He pushed it the four blocks to Dale Hinshaw's house to mow his yard. It was probably a little too early to mow, but the grass was starting to look raggedy, with clumps of high grass where various dogs had applied fertilizer over the winter.

Dale is home from the hospital, but forbidden to mow. It took Sam an hour to cut the grass. Dale's lawn isn't large, but there's a good bit of statuary to steer around—three concrete geese, Snow White and the seven dwarves, a wooden windmill, and two wagon wheels flanking the driveway.

For someone who's spent his adult years warning others of the fleeting nature of human life, cautioning them to get right with God while there is yet time, Dale seems shocked to have suffered a heart attack, as if a secret deal with God had exempted him from human frailties.

Sam finished mowing, shut off the mower, and climbed the porch stairs to visit with Dale, who was watching from the porch swing. Having saved his life, Sam now feels invested in it and has become somewhat protective. "Anything else I can do while I'm here?" he asked.

"No, that's about it. Is that a new mower?"

"Yep. Just got it."

"I'm a Snapper man myself," Dale said with a sniff.

"Uly was having a sale and I needed a mower, so I thought I'd give it a try." Sam wondered why every time he was around Dale Hinshaw, he ended up feeling the need to apologize for some indiscretion.

"Well, I suppose there's no harm done. I reckon the folks who work at Snapper can always get jobs at McDonald's."

This was starting to remind Sam of his first church, where he'd made the error of purchasing a used Toyota from his brother, Roger, causing his congregation to question his patriotism. Disinclined to subsidize treason, they stopped giving to the church and didn't resume until Sam apologized, sold the Toyota, and bought a Ford. Which, incidentally, was made in Canada, though Sam thought it best not to point that out.

"You know, Dale, we live in a global economy now."

"That's just what the Antichrist wants you to believe, Sam. Next thing you know, we'll all be wearing the mark of the beast and have computer chips under our skin. Won't be able to go anywhere without Big Brother knowing where we are."

"Just because I bought a Honda lawn mower?"

"It's from small acorns that mighty oaks grow," Dale said smugly.

Sam was starting to feel less protective of Dale with every passing moment.

"How's things going at the church without me?" Dale asked.

Superbly, Sam wanted to say, but for the sake of kindness didn't. "Oh, we're muddling through. We'll be glad to have you back."

"Don't know when that will be. Doctor told me to stay away from crowds. Said if I picked up a virus, it could go straight to my heart and I'd be a goner."

"You stay away as long as you need to," Sam said. He rose to leave. "You take care, Dale. Call if you need anything."

Sam descended the porch steps, pushed his mower down the sidewalk past Snow White and her short friends, then turned toward home. A block later, he passed Bea Majors's house. She was lifting bags of mulch from the trunk of her car, leveraging the bags up and over the lip of the trunk before letting them fall to the ground, then dragging them across the grass to the flowerbeds that ringed her home.

Sam stopped to help, even though Bea Majors was still upset with him from the month before, when he'd refused to draw and quarter Deena Morrison's fiancé, Dr. Pierce, for expressing doubts about the Virgin Birth. She'd relinquished her seat at the organ, thinking the church would rise up, fire Sam, and carry her back to church on their shoulders. That they seemed to have gone forward without a hitch is annoying her to no end.

Sam unloaded five bags of mulch, making small talk and updating Bea on the church news. She didn't have much to say, having suffered one indignity after another at the hands of the church. First, they hadn't begged her to return. Then they'd had the audacity to advertise in the *Herald* for a new organist. A paid organist, at that. Twenty dollars a week, plus twenty-five dollars for weddings and funerals, plus three weeks off a year, plus a paid membership in the Church Organists of Mid-America (COMA).

Fifty years she'd played the organ at Harmony Friends and never gotten one thin dime. But let her leave, and they'd spend money like drunken sailors. She'd been thinking of billing the church for her services. Fifty-two Sundays a year for fifty years, except in 1968, when she'd missed a Sunday to attend her aunt's funeral. As near as she could figure, the church owed her fifty-two thousand dollars, and that wasn't including weddings and funerals. If she hadn't needed her mulch unloaded, she wouldn't even have spoken to Sam, she was so worked up.

Sam spread the mulch with Bea hovering over him, pointing

out the thin spots and cautioning him not to smother the tulips, which had elbowed their way through the soil.

He complimented her tulips, which soothed her somewhat. She has been cross-pollinating her tulips, despite warnings from her sister, Opal, who believes the natural order shouldn't be trifled with and that Bea will have some explaining to do come Judgment Day.

"If you don't believe in trifling with the natural order, how come you dye your hair?" Bea had asked her.

After that Opal had piped down for a while.

"Yes, you sure do have beautiful tulips," Sam said. "I sure wish I could grow flowers like these. I just don't seem to have the knack for it."

"It's all in the soil," Bea confided. "Coffee grounds and fish heads."

"Fish heads?"

"Dale gives me the fish heads after he's cleaned his fish. I bury 'em alongside the tulip bulbs. Gotta keep the cats away, though."

"Well, it certainly appears to be working."

"I have more tulips than anyone else in town," Bea boasted.

"Even more than Fern Hampton?" Sam asked.

Bea snorted. "Fern Hampton couldn't tell the difference between a tulip and her tush. She went and bought all those bulbs at Wal-Mart last fall and slapped 'em in the ground willy-nilly, and now she's goin' around acting like the world's expert

on tulips. You just watch and see, one spring she'll get the root
rot and they'll be dead inside a week."

"You think?"

"Yes I do, and I won't shed one tear either," Bea said emphat-
ically.

Gardening, Sam was beginning to learn, was a blood sport.

He finished spreading the mulch, then stood, stretching his
sore muscles. By that time, Bea was feeling more hospitable and
scurried inside to retrieve a coffee can full of fish heads, which
she offered to Sam. "You got to keep 'em cold until you use 'em."

Sam thanked her profusely, feigning enthusiasm. He pushed
his new lawn mower around the corner and down the sidewalk
past Hester Gladden's house, then crossed the street, turned into
his driveway, and rolled the mower into his garage, maneuvering
between his sons' skateboards and bicycles. He carried the fish
heads inside and placed them in the refrigerator, then washed his
hands and took a nap.

His wife, Barbara, found them early the next morning while
Sam was still asleep. He was awakened by a shriek, then the clat-
ter of a can striking the kitchen floor. He pulled on his robe and
eased his way down the stairs and into the kitchen. A fish head
lay on the rug in front of the sink, leering up at his wife with a
bulging eye.

"What is that?" she asked.

"A peace offering, I think."

"Whatever it is, get it out of my house."

Sam picked up the fish remains, placed them in a grocery sack, and carried them out the back door, down the brick walk next to the driveway, and around behind the garage to the burn barrel in the alley. He struck an Ohio Blue Tip and lit the sack, watching as curls of flame consumed the paper.

Shirley Finchum spied him from her kitchen window, wondering what he was burning so early in the morning. Probably dirty magazines, she thought. Sneaking out to do his filthy business while everyone was still asleep. She'd never trusted Sam Gardner, not since he was in the seventh grade and she'd worked at the Rexall and caught him hiding behind the comic rack, ogling that month's issue of the *Police Gazette*.

She phoned Bea Majors. "Guess what that pastor of yours is doing?"

"What?"

"Standing out in the alley in his bathrobe up to no good."

"Is that all he's doing, just standing out there?"

"He's burning something. Dirty magazines, I think," Shirley conjectured.

"And to think I let him touch my tulips," Bea said with a shudder of disgust.

They bemoaned the lack of morality, how the town was going to Hades in a handbasket, and it was all Sam's fault.

"Did you know he's a Democrat?" Shirley asked.

"No, but I suspected as much. And to think I gave him fish heads."

Sam walked past Bea's on his way to the meetinghouse. She was out front, surveying her flowers.

"Good morning, Bea," Sam said cheerfully.

"You owe me fifty-two thousand dollars," Bea snapped.

"Excuse me?"

"And I want my fish heads back too."

Sam was going to stop, but thought better of it. He smiled, gave a little wave, and kept on walking. There are some things mere mortals are not meant to understand, and Bea Majors is one of them.

Strolling to his office, he turned his mind to more pleasant pursuits, namely, the summer stretching before him, an un-painted canvas of relaxation, when life downshifted. Sunday school ebbed to a close. Storm windows were taken out of house windows and carried to the attic and the screens set in place. The bugs were vacuumed from the window sills. Rockers and swings were hauled up from the basement and installed on the porch.

Sam passed the Dairy Queen. The sign out front read *Free Sprinkles on Every Cone* on one side and *Opening Today* on the other. His heart gave a happy leap. A new mower, summer loom-ing on the horizon, and evening walks to the Dairy Queen, where he would sit with his family on the long bench watching the cars drive past on Highway 36 while chasing sprinkles around his cone.

Three

Lost Love

*I*t was early May, and Miss Rudy was making her rounds through the town, gathering books for the annual book sale held in the basement of the library. It is the 101st anniversary of the library. When the library was built, they carved the year in Roman numerals above the doorway. Unfortunately, people don't know Roman numerals like they used to, and the 100th anniversary slipped by.

They were six months into the 101st year before Miss Rudy noticed. She promptly hired Judy Iverson to paint a banner announcing the 100th anniversary, then hung it over the Roman numerals above the doorway. She didn't mention her oversight to the Library Board. They've been looking for evidence of senility and she didn't want to give them any ammunition.

Miss Rudy's dementia is the only thing that's kept her in Harmony. If she were in full control of her faculties, she'd have left long ago for some brighter shore where people value enlightenment.

For forty-five years, Miss Rudy has waged her private war against intellectual sloth. Each new crop of town council members wants to cut the library's funding. "We already got enough books," they tell her. "Why do we need more?"

She corrects their grammar in public, which doesn't endear them to her cause. "We already *have* enough books. And no, we don't."

Lovers of the written word are viewed with suspicion in Harmony. If Shakespeare had grown up here, he'd have been told to quit goofing off and get a real job. His parents would have urged him toward blacksmithing.

Every year, Miss Rudy hopes it will be different, that when she goes forth to solicit books for the sale she will uncover a first edition of *To Kill a Mockingbird* or *The Grapes of Wrath*. Instead, she is inundated with paperback romances with titles like *Passion in Paris* or *Summer Fling*. People leave them in stacks at the book door of the library, after hours, when no one is likely to discover their depravity.

She's also swamped with back issues of *Reader's Digest,* Upper Room devotionals, and the Friendly Women's Circle cookbook. Confident it would hit the best-seller list, the Friendly Women had 5,000 copies printed in 1983 and managed to sell 432 of them. The remainder are stored in the attics and basements of Friendly Women all over town. For years they've unloaded them on Miss Rudy. They are the zucchini of books—everyone has more than they could possibly use. Miss Rudy hauls them to the recycling center in Cartersburg.

She stopped by Kivett's Five and Dime to see if Ned had any books to donate. Ned was gone, but Nora Nagle was working the checkout counter. She's been reading Emily Post's book on wedding etiquette. She isn't engaged, but wants to be prepared in case the right man happens along, though she is starting to think she might have to settle for the wrong man.

Nora Nagle was the 1975 Indiana Sausage Queen. She moved to Hollywood, where she starred as a dancing grape in an under-wear commercial, but doesn't have a romantic prospect in the world. She is too beautiful; men are frightened of her. So they ask out less attractive women while Nora Nagle sits at home. She's been thinking of marring her perfection so she won't be so intimidating, maybe breaking her nose or letting her eyebrows grow together.

She gave the wedding book to Miss Rudy for the sale, who made a mental note to set it aside for Deena Morrison. A goodly number of people have taken a deep interest in Deena's wed-ding, which is drawing perilously close. Bob Miles has been run-ning a countdown in the upper left corner of the front page of the *Herald,* next to the weather. *Seasonal temperatures expected, though variations might occur. Thirty-nine days until the big day!*

Deena found the wedding dress she wanted in a magazine at the library. Miss Rudy relaxed her rule about not letting people check out current magazines so Deena could show it to Miriam Hodge, who is sewing her wedding dress.

In the midst of all the wedding planning, Deena's computer crashed. Self-proclaimed computer healers from around town laid hands on it, trying to resurrect it, but apparently lacked faith because it's still broken. She's been using the computer at the library, trolling the Internet with Miss Rudy for wedding ideas.

Deena is having the kind of wedding Miss Rudy wishes she could have had, but never did. It isn't just the wedding Miss Rudy wanted; it's the marriage, the sharing of life. When she was Deena's age, she was caring for her parents, who'd had her late in life. After they died, she went off to college, then moved to Harmony to work at the library. The years passed, piling one on top of the other, and now she's seventy-seven and the sand has nearly run out of her hourglass.

It's tolerable in the daytime, when she's at the library. People are in and out, and there are books to shelve and the occasional teenager to rein in. In the spring, she has the book sale to occupy her attention. It's the evenings that wear her down. The library closes at seven. She turns off the lights and locks up at five after, then walks the half block to her darkened, silent house.

Across the street, she can see Owen Stout and his wife, Mildred, sitting in their chairs, talking or watching TV or playing Scrabble. Behind her, on the other side of the alley, the Grants can be seen going about their evening—the boys at the kitchen table doing their homework, Uly and his wife standing at the sink washing the supper dishes.

She'd had someone once, a long time ago. He'd moved to town to work for the phone company. They'd met at church. He moved a pew closer each week, until on the fifth Sunday he'd worked up the nerve to sit in her pew and share a hymnal. He'd stopped by the library the next day, glancing at her from the biographies. The next morning he was back, asking permission to call on her that evening.

It was late spring. He arrived at her house a little before eight. She'd hurried home from work to shower, iron a new dress, and dab perfume on her wrist. They sat on her porch swing. He'd grown up in a small town just like this one, he'd told her, then had graduated from high school, was sent to Korea, came home alive and grateful, and had been with the phone company ever since. Never married.

He visited every night for a week and sat on her porch. On the fifth night he held her hand, the next night they kissed, and two nights later she invited him inside for a game of Rummikub, even though she knew people would talk. Two months passed, he proposed, and she accepted. The date was set for early November. Then there was a car wreck. He lasted two days at a hospital in the city, all alone, before she managed to find him. He was buried the day they were to be married, in South Cemetery by the Co-op.

She has the wedding rings they bought at the jewelry store in Cartersburg. She keeps them in a jewelry box on her bureau, and at night, when she is especially lonesome, she holds them and remembers better days. She has one picture of him, which she keeps next to her bed—the picture accompanying their engagement announcement in the *Herald*. But that was a long time ago, and people have forgotten. They walk past his grave and see his name and wonder who he was and why he's buried there. No one remembers, except Miss Rudy.

She has a handkerchief he gave her the night he proposed. She was crying, and he pulled it from his pocket to dab her tears. She kept it to launder, but never got around to giving it back.

All of that came to mind while she was standing in Kivett's Five and Dime, these unbidden memories, never far from the surface.

She thanked Nora for the wedding book. When she returned to the library, she phoned Deena, asking her to stop past that evening on her way home from the Legal Grounds.

Deena knocked on her door at fifteen after eight. Miss Rudy was washing the supper dishes. She invited Deena in, poured them glasses of tea, and then gave her the book. They sat at the kitchen table, thumbing through the book and discussing the upcoming nuptials. Miss Rudy asked if she had something borrowed.

"What do you mean?"

"For your wedding day," Miss Rudy said. "You have to wear something old, something new, something borrowed, and something blue."

"Oh, that. I haven't gotten that far yet."

Miss Rudy rose from the table, walked into her bedroom, reached into the top drawer of her bureau, and pulled the handkerchief from it. She went back into the kitchen and pressed it into Deena's hand. "You can borrow this, if you wish."

Then, for reasons she still doesn't understand, she told Deena how she'd come to possess it. She regretted it immediately. Deena began to cry.

"Oh, I should never have told you. I'm sorry. I didn't mean to make you sad. Please forgive me."

"Don't be silly. I'm glad you told me," Deena said, leaning over to put her arm around Miss Rudy. "How difficult that must have been for you."

They sat that way the longest time, Deena patting Miss Rudy. A silence enveloped them. In the front room, the mantel clock ticked on, as it always had, with a certain detached cadence. Across the alley, Uly Grant yelled out the back door for his sons to come in for the night.

"Just look at us," Miss Rudy said, "sitting here being melancholy when the happiest day of your life is fast approaching. Let's be done with these silly tears."

Miss Rudy stood and smoothed out her dress, then carried the tea glasses into the kitchen. Deena rose and followed her, standing in the doorway. "I want you to be in my wedding."

"Excuse me?" Miss Rudy said.

"I would be honored if you would be my maid of honor."

"Me? Why would you want a dried-up, old woman like me in your wedding? Surely you have a young friend or a family member."

"I have a brother, but I don't think he'd look good in a dress."

"You're being silly," responded Miss Rudy, waving her hand in a gesture of dismissal.

"I am most certainly not. It's the prerogative of a bride to pick her maid of honor, and I want you. After all, you've been a great help to me."

Miss Rudy looked at Deena for a long moment. "I don't know what to say."

"Then say yes."

"You're sure?" Miss Rudy asked.

"Absolutely positive."

"Then, yes, I'll do it—provided I don't have to wear a dress that shows my cleavage. That's unseemly for a woman of seventy-seven."

"You'll be the picture of modesty," Deena promised.

Deena stayed another half hour, then excused herself to go home. It was a warm, late spring night. Miss Rudy finished washing the dishes, then went out to her front porch. Ernie Matthews had come the week before to carry her porch furniture up from the basement. She sat on the porch swing, the one she'd shared so long ago, dreaming and hoping and holding hands.

The paint had flecked off. Ernie had offered to paint it. She had thanked him, then politely declined. She wanted it just as it had been, when there was joy and life was good. The swing was bowed on the left side, where she'd always sat. She on the left, he on the right, pushing back and forth in a pleasant rhythm.

Across the street, Owen and Mildred Stout rose from their game of Scrabble at the dining-room table and walked through the house, turning off the downstairs lights. She saw the bathroom light upstairs flicker on, then five minutes later fall dark. A faint glow from Mildred's bedside table bathed the room in a soft orange. A shadow appeared behind their bedroom curtains. It was Owen, easing open the window for fresh air.

Up and down the street, windows darkened.

Miss Rudy rose and went inside, slipped out of her clothes and into her nightgown, brushed her teeth, climbed in bed, and then reached for the picture beside her bed. It had yellowed over the years and her eyes weren't as good, but she could still make him out. The strong jaw, the kind smile, the thatch of unruly hair. "Bachelor hair," he'd called it, with a laugh.

She returned the picture to her bedside table, turned off the light, and lay in the dark, remembering. They'd met forty years ago this past Sunday. Forty years. There were some dates she forgot, but not that one. Never that one.

A Present Danger

Ellis Hodge sat at his kitchen table, looking over the fields toward their pond, eating his pancakes with unusual gusto.

"You gonna help me clean off around the pond, kiddo?" he asked Amanda, reaching over to tousle her hair with a callused hand.

"Can I drive the bush hog?" Amanda asked.

He leaned back in his chair and studied her. "I don't know about that. You're awful young. How old are you now?" He was trying his best to look serious.

"I'm sixteen, you know that. And I have my driver's license."

"Oh, yes, that's right. Don't see how I could have forgotten that. We've nearly died at your hands a dozen times already."

Amanda Hodge, for all her intelligence and poise, was a menace behind the wheel. In a scant six months, she'd killed a groundhog, knocked over their basketball goal, and taken out the lamppost in front of Grant's Hardware.

"A little more practice won't hurt, I suppose," Ellis said. "Nice, level ground. No ditches or stumps. Insurance is paid up. Sure, you can drive the bush hog." He grinned.

"Don't pay him any mind," Miriam told Amanda. "You'll be a fine driver in no time at all."

"I just hope we don't run out of cars first," Ellis said with a grin.

"You stop pestering her," Miriam warned, snapping him with a dish towel.

Pestering the women in his life was something Ellis Hodge enjoyed to no end, and over the years Miriam and Amanda had learned to give as good as they got.

Amanda had been born to Ellis's no-good brother, Ralph, and his wife. Wretched alcoholics, they'd taken Ellis and Miriam's life savings on the condition they leave Amanda with them, move far away, and never return. That was five years ago, and Amanda had blossomed in their absence. Letters from colleges arrived on an almost weekly basis, urging her to apply. And to Ellis's dismay, teenage boys were starting to swarm around their doorstep like bees to honey.

It was a Saturday morning, late in May. Deena Morrison's wedding was two weeks away. Everyone had assumed the wedding would be held at the Harmony Friends meetinghouse. Though she hadn't asked to have it there, the trustees had carpeted and painted the building the winter before in anticipation of the big event. When she'd announced she was having an outdoor wedding at the Hodges' farm, in the pasture beside the pond, people were put out for a while, but got over it when Deena hired the Friendly Women's Circle to cater the reception.

The task had fallen to Ellis and Miriam to spruce up the pond. Ellis had retired to the barn the month before to build an arbor, while Amanda and Miriam had busied themselves planting ornamental grasses and a variety of flowers in clusters around the pond's perimeter. Ellis had tilled the ground around the pond, laid on grass seed, and had a thick carpet of bluegrass to show for his efforts.

"Tell you what, honey," Ellis said, finishing his last bite of pancakes. "Why don't you bush-hog the pasture so folks'll have a place to park, and I'll use the riding mower and mow off around the pond."

"It doesn't look like anyone will be mowing today," Miriam said, peering out the window. "It's starting to rain."

The rumble of thunder could be heard in the distance.

"There goes the day," Ellis grumbled.

"It doesn't have to be," Miriam said. "We've been talking forever about driving up to the city to see the new state museum. Besides, it's time we exposed Amanda to a little culture. Why don't we go today?"

"Can I drive?" Amanda asked.

Ellis was trapped, with no hope of escape. "Uh, well . . ."

"Sure you can. It'll be good practice," Miriam said.

Miriam and Amanda cleaned up the breakfast dishes while Ellis got dressed, checked the oil, and swept the straw out of the truck. He sat in the truck waiting for them to come out, putting the time to good use by praying they would reach the city alive.

Driving the back roads, it's three hours to the city. They passed through one small town after another, making a game of it, seeing who could spy the water tower first as they approached each town.

"They say those old water towers were welded with lead and now these kids are getting brain-damaged and that's what's behind all this hyperactivity," Ellis said. Ellis was a storehouse of peculiar information, most of it inaccurate. He was fond of saying, "They say . . . ," then disclosing some startling revelation, though he could never remember who the "they" was.

"That's ridiculous," Miriam said. "If that were true, they'd be tearing them down."

"I'm just telling you what they say."

"Who's this *they* you're talking about?"

"Some professor from this college out in California," Ellis said. He often attributed his sources to a professor two thousand miles away.

Amanda and Miriam began to chuckle.

"You laugh all you want, but don't blame me if you end up addlepated," Ellis cautioned. "I warned you."

"But we're on a well," Amanda said. "We don't get our water from the tower."

"There was a time when children respected their elders and didn't talk back," Ellis said. "Now pay attention to your driving. You almost hit a dog back there."

"What are you talking about?" Miriam asked. "She missed it by fifty feet. Besides, it was tied to a tree."

They bickered back and forth good-naturedly the entire way to the city. They don't have a radio in the truck. Ellis had read somewhere that sound waves from car speakers caused men to be sterile, so he'd taken it out and replaced it with commentary.

He carries a bird book in his glove compartment, which he uses to identify the various fowl who've encountered vehicles head-on and lost. On the way to the city, they pulled over for two starlings and a yellow-bellied sapsucker on its way to Canada for summer vacation.

"I wonder if birds commit suicide," Ellis mused. "Maybe just get fed up with it all and decide to eat a bumper."

This was the kind of topic that could occupy Ellis's attention for hours on end.

"What's interesting," he said, "is that I've never found a dead bluebird. Not once. I guess that song is right."

"What song is that?" Amanda asked.

"The bluebird of happiness song. You know that one, don't you?" He sang a few bars. "Be like I, hold your head up high, till you find a bluebird of happiness." He hummed the rest of the song, then said, "They got these medicines now for people who are depressed. Maybe if they mixed some of that up with the birdseed, we wouldn't have so many birds killin' themselves."

"Maybe it wasn't suicide," Amanda suggested. "Maybe they were just slow."

"Or stupid," Miriam added.

"And squirrels," Ellis continued. "You can't hardly drive a mile without hitting a squirrel. It's like they want to die. They're just standing there in the road and along you come and they run right underneath your wheels. What have squirrels got to be depressed about?"

Miriam sighed. "They're probably wife squirrels whose husbands drove them nuts."

Ellis frowned.

They stopped at a diner south of the city for an early lunch. It was still raining. Amanda parked the truck, and they hopscotched their way to the restaurant door around the pools of water that had collected in the parking lot. There was an open booth near the back. It was warm and steamy inside; the windows were fogged over. A jukebox in the corner crooned a Don Williams song.

"Well, I have to say you were right, Miriam. We needed a little culture." Ellis glanced around the diner. "This is nice. Real dishes and everything."

They ordered three cheeseburgers. "Drag 'em through the garden," Ellis told the waitress, who smiled as if Ellis were witty and clever, though she'd heard that expression fifty times a day for the past ten years.

Ellis noticed a man over at the jukebox, leaning against the glass and peering at the selections. Though his back was to him, the tilt of his head seemed most familiar. And when the man turned to a woman and asked, "How about Willie Nelson?" Ellis was sure. It had been five years, but when you grow up sharing a bedroom with your little brother for eighteen years, staying up late, talking back and forth in a moon-shadowed room, you'd know him anywhere.

Ralph Hodge turned from the jukebox and, seeing Ellis, stopped and stared. The brothers studied one another, not saying a word. Then Ralph smiled slightly, nodded at Ellis, and sat down next to his wife.

"What's wrong, honey?" Miriam asked.

Ellis tore his eyes away from his brother. "Nothing, nothing at all. Just waiting for our food, that's all."

He leaned back in the booth and draped his arm around Amanda, protectively, instinctively.

Their cheeseburgers came; they ate quickly, Ellis urging them along. "Got to see that museum before it closes. Let's not dawdle."

Ralph was the first to leave. Ellis watched as he paid his bill at the counter, then opened the door for his wife, and walked out into the rain, hunched over, toward their car, a white, rust-speckled sedan. They sat in the car. Then Ralph's wife turned in her seat and peered into the diner. Her car door opened, and she stepped out and began walking toward the diner.

Ellis watched, transfixed. She was crying, her tears mingling with the rain.

Ralph jumped from the car, caught up with her halfway across the parking lot, and guided her back to their car.

If Ellis hadn't been paying attention, he never would have heard them.

His brother saying, "It wouldn't be right."

His wife crying, "But that's our baby in there."

Miriam glanced at Ellis, then followed his gaze out the window as Ralph and his wife climbed back in the car. "Why are you staring at those people?" she asked.

"Oh, no certain reason. Just thought I knew them, that's all. Looked like some fella I used to know over at the feed store in Cartersburg. But it wasn't." He forced himself to take the last bite of his cheeseburger.

The reverse lights on Ralph's car lit up as he backed from his space, then went dark as he rolled forward, pausing at the highway before accelerating away, his car disappearing in a swirl of mist and fog.

"You girls, ready?" he asked, standing up, pulling the wallet from his back pocket, and laying down a tip.

"Let's go," Amanda said. "Can I drive?"

"How about we let Ellis do the driving now that we're in the city," Miriam suggested.

They paid their bill, then dashed to the truck. Amanda sat between them. Ellis was in no mood to stay in the city, in the vicinity of his brother. He started the truck, then turned to Miriam. "You know, I think I might have left the iron on back home."

"You haven't used an iron in twenty years," Miriam laughed. "What do you mean you left it on?"

"I unplugged it," Amanda said. "I ironed my jeans, then I unplugged it."

"I'm sure I smelled something hot just before we left," Ellis insisted. "Did you unplug the coffee pot?"

Miriam thought for a moment. "Yes. It was dirty, so I washed it. I remember unplugging it then."

"Wonder what it was I smelled?" Ellis mused. "Oh, well, it'll probably be all right. Anyway, that's why we have insurance. Right?" He moved the gearshift into reverse and backed up.

"Do you think we should go back and check on things?" Miriam asked, a note of concern creeping into her voice.

"Nah, we'll be all right. It's probably nothing."

He edged the truck forward and pulled onto the highway.

"Maybe we ought to go home," Miriam said.

"You think?"

"Yes, let's. Amanda, is that okay with you, honey?"

"I guess so. Can I drive?"

Ellis rolled to stop. "Sure, honey. You drive, and I'll keep us company."

But he scarcely said a word the whole way home. He just stared out the side window of the truck, preoccupied.

"Don't worry. The house will be fine," Miriam said, patting his hand.

"Hope so."

They turned into the driveway a little before three. Up the lane, their farmhouse stood unmolested, against a backdrop of oak trees Ellis's grandfather had planted sixty years before.

"See, everything's fine," Miriam said, with a sigh of relief.

Ellis nodded his agreement, though in his heart he knew it wasn't true.

five

The Night Before

*A*ll things being equal, Sam Gardner preferred funerals over weddings. There were no mothers of the bride to appease, no hungover groomsmen to sober up or photographers to accommodate. At funerals, the guest of honor lay quietly, without a word of protest or advice, not worrying for one moment whether he'd forget the vows or she'd trip on her bridal gown.

At funerals, he didn't have to sit in a banquet hall eating overcooked chicken with inebriated strangers. Or dance. Instead, people gathered in the church basement, in the bosom of family and friends, eating chicken and noodles, profoundly grateful for having dodged death's bullet.

Funerals didn't require a rehearsal the night before, which tended to be even worse than the wedding. Sam hated rehearsals most of all—the last minute changes in the ceremony, the frayed nerves, having to explain to a pregnant bride why "You're Having My Baby" is not an appropriate wedding song.

Despite this, he'd been looking forward to Deena's wedding ever since Dr. Pierce had proposed the autumn before. Now the week of Deena's wedding had arrived and Harmony was frantic with activity. Ned Kivett had ordered in a rack of new dresses at the Five and Dime, which was picked clean five days before the wedding. Kathy at the Kut 'n' Kurl was staying open late to accommodate the mob of women wanting their hair styled. On Thursday, a white three-spired tent appeared next to the Hodges' pond, as if the circus had come to town.

"Ellis told me they had three hundred chairs," Asa Peacock said to no one in particular at the Coffee Cup Restaurant.

"I heard they was having a swan made of ice," Kyle Weathers said. "Bet five dollars it'll be a puddle of water before noon."

"Betcha it won't," Clevis Nagle said. They each pulled a five-dollar bill from their wallets and handed it to Vinny for safekeeping in his cash register.

"How's Jessie coming with the cake?" Vinny Toricelli asked Asa.

"She's startin' on it tomorrow. I tell you, she's been busy as a one-eyed man at a go-go girl convention."

Sam Gardner had forgotten about the cake. Maybe weddings weren't so bad after all.

On Friday morning, Sam wrote his Sunday sermon—a brief meditation on the joy of marriage while people still had matrimony on their minds. The drawback to preaching in a small town is that everyone knows everyone else too well. Sam spent two hours trying to think of a couple in town whose marriage was without blemish, whose union could serve as an inspiration to the congregation.

He thought of Miriam and Ellis Hodge, but then remembered that the summer before last Ellis had to move to the barn for a month. So much for the Hodges. Then Sam remembered his grandparents, who were now deceased and therefore unlikely to divorce. Sam often waxed eloquent about dead people, knowing they wouldn't do something the next week that would necessitate a retraction.

He finished his sermon around noon, went home for lunch, then drove the back roads to Cartersburg to visit Alice Stout at the nursing home. Her room was warm and his stomach full; sitting in a rocking chair at the foot of her bed, he fell asleep. When he stirred a half hour later, Alice was still talking, so he closed his eyes for another fifteen minutes. Then he said a little prayer for Alice, thanking God for her life, such as it was, hugged her good-bye, and drove to the Hodges' for the wedding rehearsal.

It was early and he was the first to arrive, so he helped the Hodges arrange the folding chairs into rows underneath the white tent.

"This is some affair," Sam commented.

"It's simply lovely," Miriam said. Then she sighed. "Ellis and I were married at the parsonage on a Friday night after the cows were milked."

"We're just as married," Ellis pointed out. "I don't know why people go in for all this folderol."

"I'm just saying it would have been nice to have the memory."

Sam was beginning to regret he'd raised the subject and was quite relieved to see Deena and Dr. Dan Pierce turn into the driveway. They passed the barn and drove through the gate over the cattle guard, then down the pasture lane toward the pond, rolling to a stop beside the tent.

Miss Rudy was seated in the back, clutching Emily Post's book on wedding etiquette. She'd read the book three times in preparation for the big day. Dr. Pierce's best man, his only brother, sat beside her, looking rather glum. When he'd agreed to be the best man, he'd hoped Deena's maid of honor would not only be fetching, but morally indiscriminate, someone who believed in free love and living for the moment.

Instead, he'd ended up with Miss Rudy, who'd already made him spit out his chewing gum. "You're not a cow. You don't have a cud to chew. This is a wedding, not a baseball game. And there'll be no slouching either. Stand straight up, keep your hands out of your pockets, and try to look as if you have a little pride."

They were the only attendants. Deena avoided the usual custom of having every woman she'd ever spoken to serve as a bridesmaid. So it was just the four of them—Deena, Dr. Pierce, Miss Rudy, and one unhappy brother. Sam was elated. The fewer the people, the shorter the ceremony. It was almost as good as a funeral.

Deena's parents and her grandmother Mabel were the next to arrive. Deena's father had grown up in Harmony and then gone to college to become a lawyer. He'd graduated, moved to the city, married, and came home only at Christmas, just long enough to eat. Most people in Harmony didn't care for him, believing he'd risen above his station and gotten a big head. If he'd stayed home, Morrison's Menswear would still be open, selling Red Goose shoes, bib overalls, and plaid sport coats and sponsoring a Little League team, as the good Lord intended.

When Sam stayed up after the news to watch *Green Acres,* he'd occasionally see Deena's father on a television commercial for his law firm, agitating people to sue someone. He'd sent Deena to college to become a lawyer, was sorely grieved she'd spurned the law to open a coffee shop, and took every opportunity to remind her of his disappointment.

It had been his idea to have the ice swan, which was now residing in a wooden crate, packed in dry ice. As swans go, it had a rather short neck. It looked more like a large duck, which infuriated Deena's father, who'd spent five hundred dollars to have it made and delivered out from the city. He was on his cell phone within five minutes of his arrival, threatening a lawsuit if a new swan with a long neck wasn't delivered in time for the wedding.

It was obvious he had been gone too long. When people live in a small town, they learn to settle for ducks. They take their car to Logan's garage because the rear end thumps. A week later, Nate Logan phones to tell them their car is fixed. They get in the car and the thump returns a mile down the road, but the car no longer drifts to the left, so they quit while they're ahead.

People in the city have too many options. It's too easy to take their business elsewhere. But Nate has the only garage in town, and people don't want to anger him in case their car breaks down the next week and they need a tow. So they bite their tongues, pay their bills, thank Nate for his good work, then gripe about him behind his back.

The Hodges watched from the second row as Sam called the wedding party forward. Ellis leaned over and whispered in Amanda's ear, "I'll give you a hundred dollars if you elope when it comes time to get married."

"No, thank you. I want a big wedding with an ice goose," she whispered back.

"I thought that was a duck."

They both snickered. Miriam glared at them.

Sam gave his customary wedding rehearsal speech. "Remember, it's not the wedding that's important; it's the marriage. So let's relax and have fun and don't worry if anything goes wrong. If anyone makes a mistake, it'll give you something to laugh about when you're old and gray."

"Better not be any mistakes, as much as I'm paying for this

wedding," Deena's father muttered under his breath. "Five hundred bucks for a swan that looks like Daffy Duck."

Sam prayed for the Lord to bless their marriage, then put the wedding party through their paces, showing them where to stand and what to say.

"What are we doing for music?" Sam asked Deena.

"There'll be a string quartet. They had a bar mitzvah tonight, but they'll be here tomorrow an hour before the wedding," she promised.

"There goes another thousand dollars," her father muttered.

"You know what a string quartet is?" Ellis whispered, leaning into Amanda. "A banjo, two guitars, and a mandolin."

Amanda snorted, trying not to laugh out loud. Miriam elbowed Ellis in the ribs, hard. He grunted in pain. "Some pacifist you are," he said.

"And you better be thankful I'm a pacifist, or you'd be dead by now," she whispered fiercely. "Now behave yourself."

Miriam was never one to let religion get in the way of doing what needed to be done.

Sam had made his way through the introductory remarks and was now at the vows. "Okay, Dan, you'll go first. All you have to do is repeat after me. In the presence of the Lord, and before these friends . . ."

"In the presence of the Lord and before these friends," Dr. Pierce echoed.

"I take thee, Deena, to be my wife . . ."

Dr. Pierce repeated the line, staring at Deena, who appeared faint with joy.

"Promising, with divine assistance, to be unto thee a loving and faithful husband, as long as we both shall live." For someone who didn't care for weddings, Sam was stirred by the vows and felt his chin tremble.

Dr. Pierce recited the last sentence, then leaned forward and kissed Deena on the forehead.

"Curb your hormones," Miss Rudy scolded. "Sam hasn't pronounced you husband and wife yet."

The rest of the rehearsal went smoothly, and by the time they finished the sun was still two hours from setting. It was mid-June, and it didn't fall dark until almost nine o'clock. They stood under the tent going over the details for the next day. The sky in the west was lit like fire, a swirl of red and orange.

"Red sky at night, sailors' delight," Ellis said, smiling at Deena. "Looks like you'll have good weather for your big day."

"This is all so picture-perfect," Deena said. "We can't thank you enough for letting us have our wedding here. It's so beautiful."

"I even moved the manure pile," Ellis volunteered, gesturing south toward the barn. "Didn't want to be downwind of it tomorrow."

"We can't thank you enough," Dr. Pierce said. He turned to Deena. "We need to be moving along to the rehearsal dinner."

Deena turned to Miriam. "He won't tell me where it is, except that it's outside."

"I told you, we're going to the Mug 'n' Bun in Cartersburg. Root beer and hot dogs all around." He winked at Ellis, who thought root beer and hot dogs sounded pretty good.

They heard the crunch of gravel at the same time and turned to watch as a white, rust-speckled car made its way slowly up the Hodges' driveway, rolling to a stop at the sidewalk leading up to their house.

"I wonder who that could be?" Miriam asked.

Ellis reached over instinctively and put his arm around Amanda. "Probably a traveling salesman. I'll go shoo him off. Amanda, honey, why don't you and Miriam finish lining up these chairs. I'll be right back." He walked down the pasture lane around the barn and toward the house, stopping beside his brother, who was standing beside his car.

"Hi, Ralph."

"Hi, Ellis."

"What brings you this way?" Ellis asked. "I thought we had a deal."

"Sandy and I were hoping we could see Amanda," Ralph said. "It's been a long time."

"Absolutely not. That little girl is doing just fine, and I don't want anyone or anything upsetting that. Now why don't you get back in your car and go back to California or wherever it is you live."

Ralph stood silently, his head bowed, drawing a dusty circle in the gravel with the toe of his boot. He looked up. "Things have changed, Ellis. We went to AA, and we've been sober two years now. We wanted to tell you how sorry we are for all the trouble we caused. And we was hopin' to see our daughter."

"She's not your daughter anymore. You had your chance. Now please leave."

Ellis Hodge is not, by nature, a hard man, but he steeled himself, then pointed toward the road. "I'll have to ask you to get off my property."

Ralph reached in his back pocket, pulled out a thick envelope, and handed it to Ellis.

"What's that?"

"That thirty thousand dollars you gave us to leave, this here's ten thousand of it. I'll pay you back the rest of it just as soon as I can. We don't want your money. We just want to be part of Amanda's life again, that's all."

"You keep that money," Ellis said, pushing it back in Ralph's hand. "We had a deal. Now you move along and don't come back."

"Can we at least say hi to her?"

"No, you can't. It'll only upset her. Let's just leave well enough alone, Ralph. Now you be gone."

Sandy was seated in the front seat, peering across the pasture toward Amanda, tears coursing down her face.

"She'll be eighteen in two years," Ellis said. "I can't keep you from her then. But as long as I'm responsible for her, I'll be doing what I think's best." He hesitated for a moment. "Maybe when you get to wherever it is you're going, you can send her a letter."

Ralph opened the car door, got in behind the wheel, and turned the ignition key. The car coughed to life. He backed down the driveway, stopped at the end for a truck to pass, then turned onto the road and drove west, away from town. Ellis watched the whole while, to make sure he didn't return, then walked back across the pasture to the white tent, where Amanda and Miriam were finishing up.

"Who was that?" Miriam asked.

"Just some fella who got turned around. He missed the turnoff to Cartersburg, but I got him on his way."

They lowered the side flaps on the tent, then began walking toward the house.

"What's for dinner?" Ellis asked with forced cheerfulness.

"How about we go to McDonald's?" Amanda suggested. "We haven't eaten there in a long time."

"McDonald's it is," Ellis said, placing his arm across her shoulders.

"Would you look at that sunset," Miriam said. "What a beautiful day this has been."

Ellis didn't comment. He just drew Amanda closer and looked west.

"Red sky at night, sailors' delight," Amanda said. "Red sky at morning, sailors take warning."

There's a red morning coming, Ellis thought to himself. A blood-red morning.

Six

The Whole Shebang

S am Gardner's alarm jangled him awake at six o'clock. He groaned, rolled over, and flailed at the clock to silence it.

"Time to wake up," Barbara said cheerfully, raising the blinds high enough for the sun to shine directly in Sam's face.

"Go away and don't come back," Sam grumbled, burrowing under the blankets.

"I bet Dr. Pierce would never talk that way to Deena."

"Leave me alone," Sam muttered.

"It's time to get up. The wedding's today and there's lots to do. Besides," Barbara reminded him, "you told me to wake you up at six."

She pulled the blankets off Sam with a mighty tug, then yanked the pillow from underneath his head, taking off the pillowcase. "Hop up, Sam. It's laundry day and I've got to wash these sheets." She grabbed the fitted sheet, loosened it at the corners, and with a quick pull rolled Sam off the bed onto the floor.

He lay next to the nightstand, contemplating the ceiling. "I must warn Dr. Pierce what he's getting himself into."

Barbara gathered the sheets to her chest and sighed contentedly. "Don't you just love weddings? Two people starting a life together. Isn't it just wonderful?"

"Simply precious."

Barbara dumped the bundle of bedding on Sam. "Why don't you make yourself useful and start these sheets in the washer? Then maybe I'll fix you a little breakfast."

"Pancakes and sausage?" Sam asked hopefully.

"Nope, cereal."

"I bet Deena would fix her man pancakes and sausage for breakfast."

"Not after fourteen years of marriage and two children, she wouldn't."

Sam eased himself up off the floor, stretched, scratched his belly, then went downstairs to the kitchen and began rummaging through the cabinet where they kept the cereal. "Where's the Cap'n Crunch?"

"The boys finished it off yesterday. You'll have to have some of my Special K."

"How about I go to the Coffee Cup?" Sam asked.

"Fine with me. Just don't be late for the wedding. And don't forget you promised to weed the flowerbeds today."

He showered, combed his hair, sniffed the clothes he'd worn the day before, and then pulled them on. It was a radiant morning, sunny and seventy degrees, so Sam walked the three blocks to the Coffee Cup.

Heather Darnell was waiting tables, her hair pulled back in a French braid. She looked positively exquisite, and Sam was briefly tongue-tied.

"I'll have French braid," he said.

Heather looked at him, confused. "Pardon me?"

"I mean French bread, uh, French toast. With sausage, and a glass of orange juice."

"Coming right up, Sam."

He glanced around the restaurant. Though it was only seven o'clock, the place was full of refugees—men whose wives had driven them from their homes with talk of weddings and threats of chores.

Asa Peacock walked past and clapped him on the back. "You ready for the big show?"

"As ready as I'll ever be," Sam said.

"Boy, you couldn't pay me to do a wedding. I'd be afraid I'd screw up. Three hundred people staring at you, just waiting for you to make a hash of things. I don't know how you do it, Sam."

"Lots of practice, I suppose," Sam said. A pang of anxiety rolled through him, making his stomach churn.

"Yessiree, I'd worry about leaving somethin' out and ruinin' the whole shebang."

"I was at my nephew's wedding last year," Kyle Weathers said, "and the minister got so nervous, his voice box locked up tighter than a drum. Then he started hyperventilating and the next thing you know he was fainted dead away on the floor."

"Weddings didn't use to be that big a deal," Asa said. "Then they got to spending all that money and blew the whole thing out of proportion and now it's a big production and nobody better dare mess up."

By the time Heather came with his French toast, Sam had lost his appetite and asked if she had any Tums.

After breakfast, he stopped by the church to read through the wedding ceremony one more time to ease his mind. He usually did fine at weddings, unless the bride and groom deviated from the norm. He typically didn't preach at weddings and with good luck could conclude a wedding within fifteen minutes of starting.

Thankfully, Deena's wedding promised to be brief. There was no special music, unity candle, or readings from Kahlil Gibran about how if you love someone, let them go and if they return to you they are yours, but if they don't, they're with someone else, or words to that effect.

The only thing that gave Sam pause was Deena and Dr.

Pierce's asking Dale to give the closing prayer in gratitude for his loaning them his Mighty Men of God ring for their engagement. Though they'd asked him to keep the prayer brief and cheery, Sam feared Dale would get the cheery part out of the way as quickly as he could, then harangue people about living in sin. At the last wedding Dale had attended, he'd stood during the Quaker silence and spoken at length about not having to buy the cow if the milk was free.

Sam gathered up his Bible and his wedding book, then headed for home to dress for the wedding. Barbara was upstairs getting ready, and Sam's father, who had promised to babysit their sons, was in the backyard playing pitch and catch with them. Sam's mom was sitting on the couch, thumbing through a magazine.

It took Sam five minutes to pull on his suit. He ran a comb through his hair, smoothed his cowlick, then buffed his shoes with a sock. He drank a capful of Pepto-Bismol to guard against diarrhea, knotted his tie with a Windsor knot, tucked a handkerchief in his pocket, and gargled with Listerine.

They arrived at the wedding at ten-thirty, an hour early. Miriam Hodge was arranging flowers around the trellis Ellis Hodge had built for the occasion. The ice swan, despite being shaded by the tent, was sweating profusely. It looked like a duck with bladder-control issues. Kyle Weathers was standing next to it, peering at his watch and smiling gleefully. "Don't think she's gonna make it. Got another hour and a half to go, and she's leaking like the *Titanic*. Looks like Clevis owes me five dollars."

Clevis sat in the front row, a glum expression on his face. Dale was seated next to him, looking pale and worn; his tie was loosened and the top button of his shirt undone. Dolores was fanning him with the wedding announcement.

Miss Rudy was guarding the door of the farmhouse, ready in the event roving marauders happened by to molest the bride. Bob Miles was circulating among the guests and wedding party snapping pictures. It was his present to the couple, one they'd wanted to decline, but couldn't, and so were stuck with him.

Deena's parents were standing with Dr. Pierce's parents off to the side. They were discussing that day's weather, which was ideal. When they'd exhausted that topic, they moved on to discuss the weather in general—floods, blizzards, heat spells, and the like—trying to exhaust the topic so their conversation wouldn't drift toward their jobs. Like his son, Dr. Pierce's father was a doctor, and Deena's father made his living suing physicians. Kyle Weathers had bet Harvey Muldock ten dollars the day would end in blows. Between that and the melting duck, it promised to be a profitable day for Kyle.

By eleven o'clock, there was a stream of cars on the road from town, turning up the Hodges' driveway, past the barn, and into the pasture where the Odd Fellows were directing them into neat rows. The chairs began to fill from the front to the back. Deena sat in the farmhouse, awaiting the grand moment when Harvey Muldock and his 1951 Plymouth Cranbrook convertible would deliver her to her betrothed.

At precisely eleven-thirty, Harvey rose out of the Cranbrook, the Hodges' front door eased open, and Deena's father escorted her to her chariot. Harvey stood at attention and held the passenger door open. As Deena settled in her rightful place with her father beside her, his cold lawyer's heart began to thaw.

Harvey slid behind the wheel, managing somehow to look polished even in his green plaid sport coat, dark brown pants, and white shoes. The Cranbrook rolled forward, up the driveway, past the barn, and into the pasture, gliding slowly by the neat rows of cars.

For over forty years Harvey Muldock and his Cranbrook have squired scores of beautiful Sausage Queens around town, but Deena Morrison in her bridal gown made them look like common washerwomen. She wore a simple ivory dress. Kathy at the Kut 'n' Kurl had outdone herself, braiding a strand of pearls into Deena's hair.

Opal Majors leaned into Bea. "I saw a dress just like that in *People* magazine."

"A little too much cleavage, if you ask me," Bea sniffed.

The string quartet began playing Pachelbel's *Canon* as Sam, Dr. Pierce, and his brother rose from their seats in the first row and walked to the head of the tent, next to the trellis of flowers. Miss Rudy proceeded down the aisle, her eyes straight ahead, pausing for a moment next to Kyle Weathers, whose name had appeared in the *Herald* the past six weeks for overdue books. It took all her restraint not to stop and slap him. Five yards before the trellis, with a librarian's precision, she turned sharply to the left, took two steps, then turned and faced the back of the tent, where Deena stood with her father.

In the front row, Deena's mother stood. With the snap and pop of crackling joints, the wedding guests likewise rose to their feet. Sam nodded his head. Deena's father reached over and laid his hand upon Deena's, looked down, and smiled at his only daughter. They began walking toward the front. Her father looked stoic, trying not to cry, while Deena beamed with joy.

They came to stop in front of Sam, who opened his wedding book and began to read the Quaker wedding vows. "Marriage, in its deepest reading, is an inward experience—the voluntary union of personalities effected in the mutual self-giving of hearts that truly love, implicitly trust, and courageously accept each other in good faith."

He continued, wending his way through the giving of the bride, the exchange of rings, the vows, the announcement of husband and wife, and the kiss, which was just long enough to express passion but not so long that people blushed.

The moment arrived for the closing prayer. The night before, during the rehearsal, Sam had gone over it with Dale, explaining how he was to come forward after the kiss, stand in front of the blissful couple, and invite God's blessing on their marriage.

Dale squeezed past Miss Rudy. Sam stepped aside, bowed his head, and closed his eyes, looking properly reverential. Dale cleared his throat, then paused for what Sam supposed was dramatic effect. Leave it to Dale to turn the spotlight on himself, Sam thought.

Five seconds passed, then ten. Sam edged closer to Dale to nudge him just as Dale pitched forward, knocking Deena to the ground and ending up on top of her.

That's what comes from suppressing your natural urges all your life, Sam thought. Put a beautiful woman in front of Dale and he'd go crazy with lust and assault her. He and Dr. Pierce reached down to pull him to his feet. Dale's body felt lifeless; his complexion was a waxy white.

"My Lord, I think he's fainted," Dr. Pierce said.

Dolores Hinshaw screamed, while Miss Rudy helped Deena to her feet. All across the tent, people rose to their feet, straining for a better view. The men in the tent perked up considerably. Having to attend a wedding on a perfect summer day was intolerable, but this had redeemed their day considerably.

"Somebody phone Johnny Mackey to come with the ambulance," Ellis Hodge yelled, assuming the mantle of leadership since it was, after all, his pasture in which Dale had fainted.

"Here I am, right here," Johnny said, squeezing through the onlookers to crouch at Dale's side. "Is he dead?"

"I don't think so," Dr. Pierce said. He frowned. "His pulse is weak. We need to get him to the hospital." He stood, as if searching for someone, and then spied Harvey Muldock. "Get your car ready." He turned toward Sam and Ellis. "Help me lift him."

Sam grabbed Dale under his armpits while Ellis hoisted his legs. They arranged him in the backseat of the Cranbrook, elevating Dale's legs over the side of the car. Dr. Pierce squeezed in beside him. Harvey leapt in the front seat, dropped the gearshift down three notches, and gassed his car. His tires bit into the ground and then found purchase, and the Cranbrook rocketed forward across the pasture.

Sam turned and saw Dolores Hinshaw, ashen-faced and numb with fear. Deena was standing beside her with her arm around Dolores's shoulder.

"How dreadful for you," Miriam Hodge said, taking Deena's hand. "On your wedding day of all days."

"Let's not give it a second thought," Deena said. "I just hope Dale's all right."

Sam turned to Deena, "I hate to abandon you at your wedding, but I think I should take Dolores to the hospital to be with Dale."

"Of course you should," Deena said.

"Folks are getting kind of restless. Why don't we go ahead and serve the cake," Ellis suggested. He'd been eyeing the cake for the past several hours. It was his favorite—chocolate with white icing.

The last guest left around two o'clock. Jessie and Asa Peacock stayed another hour to help Ellis and Miriam gather up the trash and fold the chairs. The phone rang just as Ellis, Miriam, and Amanda walked through their kitchen door.

"Get that, could you please, honey?" Ellis asked.

Miriam picked up the phone. "Hello."

It was Sam. "It's not looking good. They're saying he won't make it," he said, his voice catching. Miriam heard a loud sob in the background.

"I've got to go. Dolores needs me. Can you get word out to folks?" he asked, then hung up before Miriam could answer.

She stood at the phone, dazed.

Ellis walked into the kitchen. "Who was that on the phone?"

"Sam. Dale's dying. I've got to call people and go be with Dolores."

She made her way to the kitchen table, sat down heavily, thought of Dale Hinshaw, and then, to her utter surprise, began to cry.

Seven
Life's a Gamble

$\mathcal{R}$alph and Sandy Hodge sat in Owen Stout's law office on a Monday morning in mid-July. Owen was suffering the aftereffects of a weekend of fishing with his brother-in-law during which he'd imbibed his share of the grape. This conversation, however, was starting to clear his head.

"You want what?" he asked them.

"Our daughter Amanda," Ralph said. "My brother has her and he won't give her back."

"How old is she?"

"Sixteen, soon to be seventeen," Sandy answered.

"Did you give Ellis custody?"

"Not really."

"What do you mean not really?"

Ralph lowered his head, clearly ashamed.

"It happened when we were drunk," Sandy explained. "It's kind of embarrassing."

Owen paused, chewed for a moment on the end of his pen, then said, "Why don't you tell me about it."

"Well, Ellis gave us some money if we promised to let her live with him," Ralph said.

"How much money?"

"Thirty thousand dollars up front and five thousand a year after that until she turned eighteen."

"So you sold your daughter and now you want her back?"

"We weren't in our right minds," Sandy said. "But that's all over with. We joined the AA and stopped drinking and found a church and got jobs and things are better now. We just want to be a family again."

"So what do you want from me?"

"We want to hire you to get her back for us," Ralph said.

Owen leaned back in his chair, deep in thought. He'd forgotten all about his headache.

"I don't think I want the job," he said after a bit. "Amanda seems happy, and Ellis and Miriam have done a good job. Technically, she's still your child, and you can get the sheriff and go fetch her. But it'll cause you nothing but trouble, and I'd advise you against it."

Sandy began to cry. "We know it was wrong, what we did. We just want another chance, that's all."

"Well, if you go charging in there with a lawyer, it'll get nasty real quick. And you'll risk turning Amanda against you. I don't think you want that. Tell you what I'll do. I'll have a word with Ellis and see if we can't arrange a visit."

"We sure would appreciate that," Ralph said. "We don't want to cause any trouble, and we don't want to hurt Ellis and Miriam either, but she is our daughter, after all."

"Maybe you should have thought about that when you had her," Owen said.

Ralph looked up, his shoulders sagging forward and his hands clasped between his legs. "Mr. Stout, there's not one bad thing you can say to me that I haven't already said to myself a thousand times."

Owen thought for a moment, staring at Ralph. "Yes, I suppose you're right," he said after a while.

"Will you help us?" Sandy asked. "We know we don't deserve a second chance, but we'd be grateful for your help."

"All I'll promise is to go see Ellis and Miriam," Owen said. "But I'm not going to institute any sort of legal action against them. If you want that, you'll have to get another lawyer."

"Thank you," Ralph said, rising to his feet and extending his hand to shake with Owen. "We appreciate your help."

"Leave your phone number with my secretary and I'll give you a call after I've spoken with Ellis."

"We don't have a phone," Sandy said. "We're staying at the tourist cabins. Number five."

"I'll knock on your door then. Until then, keep your distance from Amanda. We don't want Ellis and Miriam getting upset." Owen ushered them from his office, just as Dolores Hinshaw came through the door for her ten o'clock appointment.

She studied Ralph and Sandy, and then recognition dawned. "Ralph, is that you?"

"Hi, Mrs. Hinshaw. I read about Dale in the paper. Sure am sorry."

"Thank you."

"You're in our prayers," Sandy said, taking Dolores by the hand.

"Why don't you go on in the office, Dolores," Owen said. "I'll be with you in a moment."

"Take care, Mrs. Hinshaw," Ralph said.

"Bye, Ralph."

They left the office, and Owen followed Dolores into his office. She settled herself in the chair across his desk.

"So how are things going?" Owen asked.

"It's one day at a time," she said.

"That's all you can do."

"I can't help but think the Lord has a purpose for all this. There Dale was, deader than a doornail, and Dr. Pierce got his heart going again. Said if they'd have gotten to the hospital even two minutes later, he'd been a goner."

"I guess God has a plan for him," Owen conjectured. Owen

Stout had never been a big believer in God, but Dale's revival would have given pause to even the most callous.

"So what can I do for you today, Dolores?"

"Dale wanted me to look into getting one of those living wills, just in case the transplant doesn't go well."

"Have they found a donor yet?"

"Not yet, but we're hoping."

"Just think of it," Owen marveled. "They can take out a man's heart and put in somebody else's."

"He just doesn't want machines keeping him alive if things don't work out," Dolores explained.

"I can certainly understand that," Owen said, turning around to pluck a piece of paper from his file cabinet, then handing it to Dolores. "You need to have Dale sign this in front of two witnesses and a notary public."

"Who's a notary public?"

"Well, my secretary is one," Owen said. "And my brother, Vernley, down at the bank, and Johnny Mackey at the funeral home."

Dolores stood to leave. "Thank you, Owen. It's awful kind of you to help us. You sure there isn't a charge?"

"You don't worry about it, Dolores. You just keep a good eye on Dale."

"Folks have been so . . . so . . ." Her voice caught. "They've been so kind."

"Well, that's what we're here for, to help one another."

He walked around his desk, took Dolores by the arm, and walked her past his secretary to the front door. He stood in the doorway, watching as she climbed in her car and backed out of the space with a roar. She'd gotten her driver's permit three weeks before. Dale had always done the driving, his way of keeping her on a short leash. Now she'd unbuckled her collar and didn't seem inclined to wear it again. She goosed the gas, squealed her tires, and sped off down the street, narrowly missing Clevis Nagle, on his way to the barbershop for a trim.

Dale Hinshaw's medical condition has been the talk of the barbershop the past several weeks. Kyle Weathers began a lottery predicting the date of Dale's demise. Even though half the pot is going to Dolores, people still think it's tacky. Bob Miles wrote a scathing editorial against it, but not before betting Dale would shuffle off to glory on or around August 21. Kyle doesn't understand why people are upset. "For crying out loud, we're givin' her half the money. Just trying to bring something good out of all this bad."

"But you don't bet on people's deaths," Sam Gardner tried to explain while getting his hair cut. "It's unseemly."

"It's no different than life insurance. You buy a fifteen-year policy and you're bettin' you'll die and they're bettin' you won't. I don't see the difference."

Sam let it drop.

Sam's car was parked in the Hinshaws' driveway when

Dolores reached home. He'd been stopping by a couple times a week to play checkers with Dale. They were seated at the kitchen table. A stack of reds was piled next to Dale. He had Sam's last checker trapped in the corner and seemed inordinately pleased with his victory. He'd been winning most of their games. Dolores was beginning to suspect Sam was going easy on him.

It gladdened her to see them together. For the last five years, Dale had railed against Sam and just this past spring had tried to get him fired. But somewhere along the way they'd forged a truce and Sam began stopping by with his checkerboard. At first it had been awkward, but now it was the highlight of Dale's day. On Mondays, he brought Dale a cassette tape of the Sunday service, which they listened to together, pausing the tape now and then for commentary.

Today was tape day, so after their game of checkers, Sam turned on the tape player. Bea Majors is back on the organ after her three-month strike over Sam's refusal to crack down on the freethinkers, so Dale and Sam winced their way through her prelude, then listened to Sam's opening prayer.

"Nice prayer," Dale said. "I liked that part about God keeping watch over the sparrows."

"Why, thank you, Dale," Sam said after a moment, caught off guard by Dale's charity.

Then they listened to the opening hymn. Sam had brought a hymnal so they could sing along—Dale in his high, reedy voice, Sam filling in the low places. Since Dale came home from the hospital, Sam has been letting him pick the hymns for worship, to help him feel a part of things. He brings Dale a church bulletin and points out his name on the prayer list.

After the first hymn is the children's message, which this week was delivered by Jessie Peacock. "What has a bushy tail and gathers nuts?" she asked.

There was silence as the children considered her question. Then Jessie called on Andy Grant, Uly's youngest son. "I know the answer's supposed to be Jesus," he said, "but it sure sounds like a squirrel to me."

They could hear the laughter of the congregation, and Dale chuckled.

Then it was time for Sam's sermon, which Dale didn't critique, though he did flinch at several points. The rest of the tape was mostly silence, it being Quaker worship. With Dale gone, no one else stands to contradict the sermon. They listened to the silence, hearing the slight hiss of the tape moving along the rollers and over the head. Every now and then they could hear Harvey Muldock clear his throat, which was his way of hinting that the silence had gone long enough. Then came the offering with Bea playing "We Give Thee but Thine Own," which is never very much since most of the members are not tithers. Sam gave the closing prayer, asking God to be with them through the week, guiding their footsteps in paths of righteousness, which Dale amened, and worship was over.

Sam reached over to shut off the tape player. "See you Wednesday, Dale," he said.

"If I'm still around." Dale had become increasingly fatalistic in the past few weeks.

Sam said good-bye, then let himself out. He had a Library Board meeting to attend. He was the president of the board, ever since Owen Stout had tricked him into it two years before. Seventeen years of ministry had made him politically wily, but he still couldn't outfox a lawyer.

He parked in the funeral home parking lot, walked across the street to the library and down the stairs, and began making the coffee. Owen Stout came in minutes later. They exchanged greetings, and then Owen said, "You might want to stop past and visit the Hodges sometime soon."

"How come? What's going on?"

"Probably ought not say."

It irritated Sam to no end when people did this—hint that someone in his congregation might be having a problem without revealing the details. Sam always thought the worst. "Is Miriam's cancer back?" he asked Owen.

"No, nothing like that."

"Well, then, what is it?"

"Can't say. It's confidential. I just thought you'd want to know."

"Know what? You haven't told me anything."

"Just keep an eye peeled that direction," Owen advised.

The others soon arrived, and the board meeting began. Miss Rudy was happy to report that the annual book sale had netted $113.26, which they'd used to have Ernie Matthews paint a new sign for the library. He'd delivered it that very morning. "I haven't even seen it," Miss Rudy said. "I thought we could all see it together." It was standing the corner with a blanket draped over it, which Miss Rudy whisked off with a flourish. *Harmony Public Librery*, it read.

They studied the sign. "I wasn't aware there was an *e* in *library*," Sam said.

"Why don't we put it up and see how long it takes someone to notice?" Owen suggested.

Miss Rudy didn't say a word, though her displeasure was obvious. Ernie Matthews was a dead man walking.

On that high note, the meeting ended. Sam left his car at the funeral home and walked the two blocks to the meetinghouse. As he passed Kyle Weathers's barbershop, Kyle flagged him down. "Is Dale dead yet?"

Sam glanced at his watch. "As of an hour ago, he was still alive."

"Sure you don't want to get in on this?" asked Kyle. "The pot's up to a hundred and fifty-three."

"No, thank you, Kyle."

"Well, would you do me a favor?"

"If I can," Sam said.

"Tell Frank he lost."

"Frank? Please tell me our church secretary didn't bet a dollar when one of our members would die."

"He didn't," Kyle said.

Sam sighed with relief.

"He bet ten dollars. Yep, got to pick ten dates. But today was his last day, so if he wants to stay in the pool, he'll need to stop past to pay up. Can you tell him that?"

Sam walked on to the meetinghouse, his mind awhirl. His secretary on a gambling binge, trouble brewing at the Hodges, a church member a heartbeat from death, and a misspelled library sign. It was just like his grandma used to tell him—trouble never rode into town alone.

Eight

The Revelation

The rest of the month whizzed past in a blur, as summer months have a way of doing. Oscar and Livinia Purdy at the Dairy Queen had a Peanut Buster Parfait sale the last weekend of July, and the floodgates opened. The lines were twenty deep, a mob of boisterous people. Bernie the policeman was pacing back and forth, his right hand twitching on his pistol grip. Large crowds made him nervous. Someone, he just knew it, was going to get shot before the day was over. Probably one of the skateboarders, Bernie thought, who were clustered at the end of the bench that ran the length of the building, every now and then looking up from their Peanut Buster Parfaits to sneer at the crowd.

"Would you look at those kids," Kyle Weathers grumbled to himself while waiting his turn. "That right there is what's wrong

with this country. You can't hardly tell the boys from the girls."
Kyle has dreams of tying teenage boys to his barber's chair and
buzzing their scalps with his electric clippers, of long strands of
hair falling to the floor and piling high around the base of the
barber's chair. He trembled with joy just thinking of it.

He surveyed the crowd, looking at haircuts. He could tell at a
glance the men whose wives cut their hair. No taper on the back
side. Their hair was the same thickness, the edges ragged, as if
bowls had been set atop their heads and the excess hacked away
with hedge clippers, like Moe in *The Three Stooges.*

Other men had been to Kathy at the Kut 'n' Kurl. He'd raised
the matter with Kathy numerous times, how no woman ever
came to his shop to get her hair cut, and if one did, he wouldn't
cut it, but here Kathy was cutting men's hair and trying to run
him out of business and rejecting the law of God, who'd made
half the world men and the other half women so's a town could
have a barbershop and a beauty parlor and both of them would
do just fine if they'd only stick with their own kind.

It hadn't done a bit of good.

To top it off, his best customer, Dale Hinshaw, was near
death. Dale was money in the bank. A haircut and neck shave
every Saturday morning, plus he bought a jar of pomade each
month and had his nose and ear hairs clipped every Wednesday
morning. Dale had the best groomed ears in town. There were
men in this town with so much hair sprouting from their ears
they looked like great horned owls. It drove Kyle to distraction.

Say what you would about Dale Hinshaw, he was neatly trimmed.

Ellis and Miriam Hodge were in line behind Kyle. Miriam cut Ellis's hair, except at Christmas and Easter, when he came to Kyle to get it fixed. Amanda was with them. The skateboarders were ogling her. Homely as a child, with big teeth, she has recently grown into them and is now cute on her way to beautiful. She'd gotten her hair styled too, probably by Kathy, Kyle thought bitterly.

Kyle was studying Vernley Stout's hair, which didn't take long as there wasn't much to study. Vernley began losing his hair at age twelve and is now reduced to a thin halo, which he trims himself.

It just isn't fair, Kyle thought. Men went bald and didn't need haircuts but once every couple months, while women's hair grew like weeds. Plus, women lived longer than men. Two years on the average. That was an extra twenty-four haircuts right there, minimum. And Kathy at the Kut 'n' Kurl got every dime of it.

A loud screeching noise and a barrage of protests from the skateboarders took his attention away from his sad plight. He glanced over to see Dolores Hinshaw whip her car into an empty space. Skateboarders were scattered in her wake. Though none appeared mangled, they were obviously shaken, their pale faces contrasting sharply with their black T-shirts.

Dolores flung open her car door, leaving a sizable crease in the car parked next to her. She eased out of the car, smoothed her dress, and made her way to the lines, gauging which one might be shorter. She stepped into Kyle's line, behind the Hodges. Kyle smiled and nodded. Good public relations for the wife of his best customer.

"Hi, Dolores," Miriam Hodge said, reaching over for a quick hug. "How's Dale?"

"A little stronger each day," she reported. "His appetite's picking up. He's been pestering me all day for a Peanut Buster Parfait."

Kyle was delighted. This was good news of the highest order. The pot was at two hundred dollars and climbing. He turned and smiled at Dolores. "You want that I come over and give Dale a haircut and shave? I can be there first thing tomorrow."

"Oh, don't bother, Kyle. Kathy came by the day before yesterday to drop off a pie, and she tidied him up. But thanks just the same."

His best customer a turncoat. Sold his soul for a piece of pie.

Dolores turned back to the Hodges. "I bet you're glad to have Ralph back home. I saw him at Owen Stout's office. I didn't know he'd come home."

Miriam and Amanda looked up, startled. Ellis appeared uneasy. He opened his mouth to speak, then decided against it. Miriam glanced at Ellis, who smiled weakly.

Dolores went on, oblivious to their reaction. "What's it been? Five years or more that he's been away?"

Ellis nodded.

Amanda stared at Dolores, open-mouthed.

Miriam, trying hard not to betray her shock, said, "It's been nice having them back, but enough about us. What can we do to help you and Dale?"

Dolores thought for a moment. "Sam's been mowing the yard, but he said he'll be going on vacation in a few weeks. Maybe we could hire Ellis to mow it."

"Don't be silly. Ellis would be happy to do it. He wouldn't think of taking your money. Would you, honey?"

Ellis was trying to shrink into the sidewalk. Miriam gave him a discreet kick in the ankle and a you're-in-deep-trouble-Mister smile. "Wouldn't you be happy to mow the Hinshaws' yard?"

"Sure, I can mow your yard. You just give me a call."

Kyle Weathers, who'd been eavesdropping on their every word and was now on the scent of a new customer, turned to Ellis. "You tell your brother that new customers get their first haircut free."

Ellis thought for a moment. "I think his wife cuts his hair."

"What is it with this town, anyway?" Kyle grumped. "Griping all the time about having to go to Cartersburg to buy anything, but won't support their local businesses."

Five minutes later, the Hodges were climbing in their truck, Peanut Buster Parfaits in hand. Ellis pulled out onto Main Street. "So when were you going to tell me my parents had come home?" Amanda asked.

"Yes," Miriam asked, "when were you going to tell us?"

"I didn't think it was all that important," Ellis said.

Miriam, normally a peacemaker, reached up and smacked Ellis on the back of the head, causing his nostrils to be buried in peanuts, chocolate sauce, and ice cream. "What do you mean, it's not important? Of course it's important. Have you spoken with them?"

Ellis wiped his face with a napkin, then decided to make a clean sweep of everything. "Just once. They came out to the house the night of the wedding rehearsal wanting to see Amanda. I asked them to leave, told them that no good could come from it. Then last week Owen Stout called to tell me they were in town and they wanted to see you, but I told him no."

"Shouldn't that have been my decision?" Amanda asked angrily. "They're my parents. Everyone knows my mom and dad are in town except me. You know how that makes me feel? Where are they staying?"

"I'm not sure," Ellis said, as they neared the tourist cabins on the edge of town. A rusty, white car was parked in the gravel lane that ran between the cabins. Whatever they had done with the money he'd mailed them each year, it was obvious they hadn't spent it on their car. The rear bumper was crumpled and the rust holes so large and numerous Ellis was surprised the vehicle hadn't collapsed in a mound of corrosion. He accelerated and passed the tourist cabins as quickly as he could.

They drove on in silence. One mile, then two. They came within sight of the trailer where Ralph and his wife had lived five years before. Theirs was the next driveway, but Ellis wanted to keep on driving, far away, on to Illinois, through Missouri and Kansas, and into Colorado. And never come back. Start all over somewhere else, where Ralph and Sandy would never find them.

He and his father had driven it once, the summer Ellis had graduated from high school. It had been his dad's idea. The crops were planted, and the summer months stretched before them, an unbroken expanse of time. He'd proposed it on a Monday morning at the breakfast table and by noon they were sixty miles west of their farm, on Highway 36, crossing over into Illinois in their Ford pickup. They camped that night outside Hannibal, Missouri, pitching their tent in a farmer's field, staying up late into the night, cooking over a fire, watching an occasional stray spark rise from the flames and ascend to the heavens.

The next day they reached Lebanon, Kansas, the geographic center of the lower forty-eight states, and paid twelve dollars to stay the night in a tourist home a block off Main Street. Ellis still remembered the high mahogany double bed with the crisp, white sheets, the worn, Oriental rugs over the polished hardwood floors, and the clawfoot bathtub. Twelve dollars for a room, supper, and breakfast. After breakfast, they drove north to the marker and stood beside their truck in the center of the United States while a man took their picture. Ellis still had the picture, sitting on his chest of drawers. He saw it every morning when he pulled out a fresh pair of skivvies.

Ellis and his father reached Denver the next day and stayed at the Brown Palace Hotel that night, which reduced them to paupers. The rest of the trip they camped out. They drove home on U.S. 40, the National Road, stopping in Independence, Missouri, to shake hands with Harry Truman, who was shorter than they'd imagined. They pulled in the driveway late Saturday night, in time for church the next morning, which had been Ellis's mother's only stipulation. That, and not to get themselves killed.

Ellis has never forgotten the trip. It is the farthest he's been away from home. Every now and then, while sitting on his front porch of a summer evening, he watches an occasional car speed west on Highway 36 and yearns to follow it, to retrace his steps from years before. Maybe see if the tourist home in Lebanon, Kansas, is still open and what it costs to stay the night in the Brown Palace Hotel.

He was thinking about it again as he pulled into the driveway with Miriam and Amanda. He considered taking Amanda away for a week or two, just the two of them, like he and his dad had done. And when they returned home, Ralph and Sandy would be gone, and their problems with them.

Their dog came running from the porch and trotted alongside the truck until Ellis rolled to a stop underneath the oak tree next to the clothesline. He turned off the engine, and they sat in the truck, quietly, listening to the engine clicking as it cooled.

"I think they're staying at the old tourist cabins," Ellis said after a while. He turned to look at Amanda. "Would you like me to go back and tell them you'd like to see them?"

She thought for a moment. "I just don't want to be kept in the dark, that's all. I'm old enough to be told these things."

Miriam reached over and patted her on the knee. "We know you're old enough, honey. You're a fine young lady, and we're very proud of you. This is just new ground for us, and we need to feel our way along. Ellis did what he thought was best."

"That's all I was doing," Ellis echoed.

Their dog was sitting next to the truck, studying them. The sun was setting in the western sky, a swirl of reds and yellows. The bullfrogs and crickets were starting their evening song.

"Maybe we could have them over for supper one night soon," Amanda said hopefully.

"We surely can," Miriam said. "How about the day after tomorrow? Ellis will go invite them first thing tomorrow. We'll have supper. Then we can sit on the porch and visit, and you can tell your mom and dad everything you've done. I'm sure they'd want to know. We can do that, can't we, Ellis?"

"We sure can," Ellis said, trying to sound sincere.

"It isn't that I don't appreciate all you've done for me," Amanda said. "I just want to see my mom and dad, that's all."

"I just don't want you to be hurt again," Ellis said, reaching over and pulling her to himself.

"Maybe they've changed," Amanda said. "Maybe they're not drinking anymore."

"That would be wonderful," Miriam said, "but you probably shouldn't get your hopes up."

They made their way inside. Amanda went straight to her bedroom. Ellis and Miriam came back outside to sit on the porch swing.

"Just what did Ralph say to you?" Miriam asked, when they were alone.

"That he and Sandy were going to AA, had found a church, and straightened out their lives."

"Don't you believe him?"

"My brother would lie to the pope to get what he wanted," Ellis said. "If they want Amanda back, it's only because they've found some advantage in it. I wish you hadn't told her we could have them for supper."

"Ellis, you know how teenagers are. If we forbid her to see them, she'd be bound and determined to. This way, it'll be in our home with us there."

Ellis thought about that for a moment. "Yes, I suppose you're right."

Miriam stood and leaned over to kiss Ellis on the forehead. "I think I'll go check on Amanda. Are you coming in?"

"Not yet."

He sat on the swing, reflecting on that day and dreading the next one, wondering how much money it would take this time for Ralph to go away.

Nine

The Stories Never Told

I t was the second Tuesday in August, the height of vacation season, and the Harmony town square was nearly deserted, except for Fern Hampton, who was waddling past the *Harmony Herald* building on her way to the grocery store. Bob Miles was perched in his office chair, staring out his front window, seeking fodder for that week's "Bobservation Post" column. Fern does her trading every Tuesday in the hope Bob will mention her in his column, which he invariably does. *Fern Hampton is on her way to the Kroger, where this week's special is ground beef at $1.25 a pound.*

He watched Sam Gardner come out of Grant's Hardware and walk by the Legal Grounds Coffee Shop, where he stopped, rattled the doorknob, then pressed his face to the glass and peered in. *The Legal Grounds Coffee Shop remains closed,* Bob typed dutifully.

At that very moment, the owner of the Legal Grounds, Deena Morrison, was eating lunch with her husband of thirty-two days and wondering if she'd made a dreadful mistake.

Their honeymoon had been a joy. Just the two of them in Belize, evening walks on the beach, scuba diving in the morning, and shopping in the afternoon. Fourteen blissful days, only to return home and learn that Dr. Pierce's mother had left her husband and moved in while they were gone. She'd taken over the master bedroom and was chain-smoking at the kitchen table, badgering Deena about keeping her maiden name.

Dr. Pierce, it turned out, was a wimp where his mother was concerned. Deena wasn't sure whom she would kill first—her husband or her mother-in-law. Worse yet, their love life had dried up. With his mother just down the hallway, Dr. Pierce's libido had gone south. Deena had even come to bed one night wearing her honeymoon bikini, to no avail. For all the effect it had, she could have worn chest waders.

"I'm going back to work on Monday," she said one Saturday night as they lay in bed.

"Who'll keep my mother company? We can't leave her alone. She's depressed."

"Well, honey, she's your mother, so if you're worried about her, why don't you stay home?"

Dr. Pierce had stared at her for a long moment. "Whatever happened to the nice, thoughtful Deena I married?"

"She's right here. She just didn't agree to a package deal.

Now are you going to help your mother find an apartment or should I?"

"You would throw my mother out on the street?"

"Did I say that? No, I didn't. I said we could help her find an apartment. She can stay one more week, but no longer," Deena warned. "Our marriage won't stand a chance if it's a threesome."

The next morning, after church, she sought Sam's counsel. He'd read of a similar situation in "Dear Abby." "I think your husband needs to put his foot down," he advised. She'd rolled her eyes at that. A bad sign. She'd been married less than a month and was already rolling her eyes.

Then, as Deena sat there in the meetinghouse office, inspiration struck. "How long has it been since you and Barbara went somewhere without the boys?" she asked.

Sam leaned back in his chair and thought. "Well, there was that morning at the Holidome in Cartersburg the week after Easter. Before that, oh, I don't know, maybe ten years. Why?"

"Why don't you take her someplace nice for a few days and let the boys come stay with me?"

"Let me get this straight," Sam said. "You're willing to watch our children so Barbara and I can go somewhere by ourselves?"

"Absolutely. It'll be fun."

Sam reached across to shake her hand before she changed her mind. "It's a deal."

The next morning, at eight o'clock, the Gardners deposited their sons at Deena's front door. At nine o'clock, Kivett's Five and Dime opened, and by nine fifteen Deena had purchased a set of drums and a trumpet. At precisely eleven o'clock, Dr. Pierce's mother was backing her Lincoln Town Car out of the driveway and heading toward home.

The following day was a Tuesday. Deena left for the Legal Grounds after breakfast, the Gardner boys in tow. As they rounded the corner in front of the hardware store, Bob Miles spied them and watched as Deena unlocked the door of the Legal Grounds, raised the blinds, and turned the sign from *Closed* to *Open*. Bob began to type. *Good news for all you coffee lovers, Deena Morrison is back to work at the Legal Grounds with two new helpers.*

As for Deena, she was inordinately pleased. She'd scarcely been married a month and had already trumped her mother-in-law. Now she just had to whip her husband into shape and she'd be set.

Somewhere, Bob knew, there was a story. Though not one he'd ever hear. The town's more interesting stories seldom find their way into the *Herald*. At one time, Bob had dreams of stumbling upon a big story and splashing it across the front page. But now his knees hurt, so he prefers to sit at his desk and let the news come to him.

Recently, however, he'd summoned the energy to snoop around. The month before, he'd seen Ralph and Sandy Hodge walk past the *Herald* building on their way to Owen Stout's office. Bob had graduated with Ralph, but he wouldn't have recognized him if it hadn't been for the Hodge duckfoot. Bob had first noticed it in the third grade, when he and Ralph had lined up alphabetically to walk to the lunchroom. It was a small class; there were no I's, J's, K's, or L's. You watch a kid duckfoot his way down two flights of stairs and a hallway every weekday for nine months and it's lodged in your mind forever.

The Hodges had stayed in Owen Stout's office forty-five minutes. He'd timed them. After that, he saw them around town from time to time, back at Owen's office, at the Dairy Queen one evening, turning into the tourist cabins, and once at the Kroger.

He'd tried to weasel information out of Owen Stout at their next Odd Fellows meeting, but Owen wasn't talking. Then he'd phoned Ellis to see what was going on, but had been told, in no uncertain terms, to mind his own business, which he had no intention of doing.

On the hunch that pastors knew a lot of secrets, Bob had dropped by the meetinghouse to visit Sam, but he was gone, out of town with his wife, Frank the secretary informed him. "And what a shame that is. Just when you wanted to get right with the Lord for all the lies you've printed, the pastor's gone. I hope you don't die before he gets back. I'd hate to see a man have to stand before St. Pete with your load of sin."

"No, it's nothing like that," Bob said. "Say, maybe you could help me. Have Ralph and Sandy Hodge been coming to church?"

"Yes, but not this one. The secretary at the Harmony Worship Center told me they've been going there."

Frank was plugged into the town's church secretary network and consequently had the dirt on everyone.

Curiouser and curiouser, Bob thought. The Harmony Worship Center. Then it dawned on him. Maybe they were religious fanatics who kidnapped children. He'd heard about this happening in California, where they had all the cults. Who would have thought it? Little duckfooted Ralphie Hodge had gone off the deep end. Now that he thought about it, Ralph had lived in California. Ellis had told him so himself when Amanda had come to live with him and Miriam.

Now they were back, hanging out at the Harmony Worship Center and up to no good.

He phoned Ellis as soon as he'd figured it out. "You better watch out for that brother of yours. He's come back to kidnap Amanda. He was a member of a cult back there in California. They steal kids and brainwash them."

Ellis wasn't the least bit surprised.

He and Miriam had put off inviting Ralph and Sandy over for dinner, even though they'd promised Amanda they would. Unbeknownst to them, she'd been meeting with them on Saturday mornings. It had started innocently enough. She and Miriam had come to town for their weekly grocery shopping. While Miriam was at the Kroger, Amanda had walked over to the Dairy Queen and there they were, her mother and father, sitting on the bench eating ice cream cones. It had been awkward at first, but they'd agreed to meet the next Saturday morning, and it had gotten easier each week.

They'd apologized for leaving her, for their drinking, for the years of neglect. Then came the tears. Ralph and Sandy hugging Amanda, crying over the wasted years. It embarrassed Oscar Purdy to watch them, so he let them meet in the little shack behind the Dairy Queen, where the Dilly Bar freezers were.

Amanda had much to tell them: winning the National Spelling Bee, traveling to Atlanta for the Future Problem Solvers of America's annual convention, making the A honor roll every semester, getting her driver's license, and planting flowers with Miriam for Deena's wedding.

They told her how they'd gone to church, gotten saved, and stopped drinking. How Ralph was working at the glove factory in Cartersburg and Sandy was working at the Wal-Mart in Amo, and how they hoped to move out of the tourist cabins and into a real house with an extra bedroom so Amanda could come and maybe stay the night.

They couldn't visit long. It took Miriam forty-five minutes to buy groceries, so they had only a half hour. But they made the most of it. Amanda told them about her week, and they hugged her close and told her how proud they were of her, that she'd be the first woman president.

"Where do you want to go to college?" Ralph asked one Saturday. "A smart girl like you ought to go to Harvard or Yale. If that's what you want, you just say the word. I'll work three jobs if I have to."

"No, I think I want to go to Purdue and maybe become a teacher," Amanda said.

"You'd be the best teacher this world has ever seen," Sandy said. "You're so smart. You were reading by the age of three. Did you know that?"

No, she didn't. In fact, she knew hardly anything of her childhood. So they told her. Her first word, her first steps, her favorite teddy bear, which they brought to her one Saturday. She hid it in her closet, behind a cardboard box that held her winter clothes, which is where Miriam found it in early September when the thermometer dipped into the low forties and Amanda needed a long-sleeved shirt.

She'd asked Amanda about it after supper, when Ellis was out herding the livestock into the barn for the night and they were about to do the dishes.

"I'd rather not talk about it," Amanda said.

"Well, that's your prerogative, I suppose." She smoothed Amanda's hair. She hesitated. "So how are your mother and father?"

"How would I know?"

"You've been meeting them at the Dairy Queen on Saturday mornings." She pulled Amanda to her. "It's a small town, honey. And some people like nothing more than to tell everything they know."

"Now I suppose you won't let me see them," Amanda said.

"Not at all. They're your parents, and you're almost an adult." Besides, you've never given us any reason not to trust you."

"What about Ellis? Does he know?"

"Not yet."

"When were you going to tell him?"

"I think he should hear it from you," Miriam said. "That is part of what it means to grow up. You talk openly and honestly with people."

"What if he doesn't let me see them?"

"I don't think he'd do that," Miriam said. "If he does, I'll have a talk with him."

"What if I want to go live with them?"

"Let's take one step at a time. Besides, you'll be going off to college before you know it, and it'll be a moot point. Now, why don't I wash and you dry and put away?"

"It's a deal," Amanda said, reaching in for a hug.

Had it ended there, it would have been fine. Amanda could have seen her parents, Ellis would have eventually come around, and the family would have healed. Except it had been a slow summer for news, sales of the *Herald* were lagging, and Bob Miles couldn't resist the temptation to write a story about children being kidnapped by religious kooks, some of whom lived right under our noses, maybe even at the tourist cabins. So when Amanda worked up the nerve to tell Ellis she'd been visiting her parents, he went ballistic and tried to ground her to her bedroom until she married or turned sixty, whichever came first.

"I'll work on him," Miriam told Amanda. "Don't fret. A man might think he's the head of the house, but the woman is the neck that turns the head."

But Ellis wouldn't budge. He was on Amanda like robes on the pope, shuttling Amanda back and forth to school, not letting her out of his sight except to use the bathroom. Miriam tolerated it for three days before cuffing Ellis upside the head, in a gentle, Quakerly sort of way, and ordering him to settle down before they lost Amanda for good.

Bob Miles watches from his window and writes what everyone already knows, that Fern Hampton shops on Tuesday mornings and Deena is back to pouring coffee at the Legal Grounds. But sometimes it's the stories never told in the *Herald* that matter most. A mother and father longing for a second chance, talking with their daughter on a Saturday morning at the Dairy Queen. From a certain angle, the child favors the woman. They sit side by side, holding hands, thumbing through an album, the girl pointing out a snapshot on one page and a blue ribbon on the next. The woman wipes away a solitary tear and draws the girl to her. The father looks on, his hand resting on the child's shoulder.

People drive past and try to place them. Amanda, of course, they know. The National Spelling Bee Champion. The smartest kid to ever hit town. It's the man and woman they're not sure of. They'll mention it on Sunday morning at church.

"Who was that I saw you with yesterday morning?" they'll ask Amanda.

"Those are my parents," she'll say. It is a knife to Ellis's heart. He stiffens and turns away.

That's the big story in town this late summer, whispered from house to house, confided over cups of coffee at the Legal Grounds. These are mostly good people; they feel slightly ashamed of their curiosity, but they can't help it. To not spread the story would be like passing a car wreck without slowing down to stare. So around and around the story goes and where it stops, no one knows.

Ten

A Nearly Perfect Day

abor Day found the children back in school and people returning to church. Sunday school had resumed at Harmony Friends Meeting after a three-month respite from Christian education, which most of them could ill-afford. Certain other Christians in town wonder aloud what it must be like to love the Lord only three-fourths of the year, but the Harmony Friends aren't fazed by sarcasm. The Sunday after Memorial Day they shut down Sunday school, begin worship an hour earlier, and let the censure roll off their backs.

Every now and then a new member, aflame with pious zeal, will stand the Sunday before Memorial Day and harangue them for coasting through the summer. He (it's always a he) will read from Revelation about being lukewarm and warn that God will spew them out of his mouth. The old-timers sit stoically in their pews, unfazed by this moist and gruesome prophecy.

The Tuesday after Labor Day, Sam Gardner walked his sons to school. Levi was in fifth grade, Addison in third. They attend the same school, the one Sam attended, three blocks south of the town square; it's a squat brick building that appears unfinished, which, in fact, it is. The town ran out of money after three stories and had to leave off the fourth floor and the clock tower. Consequently, no one in Harmony is ever sure of the time, except when Darrell Furbay, the fire chief, sounds the fire whistle at noon. How he knows the correct time is something of a mystery.

After depositing his sons in their classrooms, Sam walked to the meetinghouse, stopping by the Legal Grounds for a cup of coffee, his third of the day. He would be visiting Dale Hinshaw later in the morning and needed extra caffeine to steel his resolve. Though Dale's brush with mortality had softened him, he now appears to have returned to his former sanctimonious self. The Sunday before, he had publicly rebuked Sam for reading the offertory prayer from a sheet of paper, instead of trusting the Lord to give him the words, as he had promised in Matthew 10:18–20: "When you are dragged before governors and kings for my sake, do not be anxious for how you are to speak or what you are to say; for what you are to say will be given to you in that hour; for it is not you who speak, but the Spirit of your Father speaking through you."

"Is his car in the garage?" Morey asked.

They peered through the window, and there sat Harvey in his Cranbrook. Sam tried opening the garage doors, but they were locked from the inside.

"Wonder what he's doing in there?" Sam asked, tapping on the glass.

"I seen a movie once where this fella locked himself in a garage and killed himself," Morey said. "Sure hope he didn't do that. It's hard to get the stink out of a car once somebody dies in it. Remember Ralph York? Had a heart attack in his school bus in '67 and we didn't find him until the next Monday morning. Had to sell the bus to a country-western band, it stunk so bad."

"I don't think the engine's running," Sam said. He tapped on the window again, this time louder and with more urgency.

"Maybe he's dead already. Maybe he had a heart attack. Stand back and I'll kick in the door."

Sam pounded on the door, next to the jamb. The old door rattled in its frame. Startled, Harvey turned and looked at them.

"He's moving," Sam said.

They heard the door of the Cranbrook open with a metallic screech, then close with a dull thud. Harvey swung open the garage doors and stared at them. His eyes were red and puffy, as if he'd been crying.

"Hey, Sam." He didn't acknowledge Morey.

"Hi, Harvey. How you doing?" Sam asked.

"Okay, I guess."

"We came to get you for the parade."

"Not going. It appears they want someone else." He glanced at Morey, finally acknowledging his presence.

"I thought we was gonna do it together," Morey said. "Me and you and Addie in the Cranbrook."

"Over forty years I've been leading the parade and now they just cast me aside like yesterday's newspaper, without so much as a how-do-you-do."

Sam had been coddling people all week and was growing weary of it. "Harvey Muldock, there's a young Sausage Queen down at the school who's been waiting for this day all her life. And here you are, throwing a temper tantrum. You oughta be ashamed of yourself."

"Aw, Sam, don't be so hard on him," Morey said. "Tell you what, Harvey. Why don't you do the driving. I don't need to be in the parade."

Harvey reddened, clearly embarrassed. "No, that's all right." He paused. "Just not easy getting old, I guess. You're not much good to anyone but doctors and morticians."

"Well, we sure need you," Sam said, softening. "Everyone's waiting for you. They won't start the parade until you're there."

"Then we better get going, men," Harvey said, straightening his shoulders. "Let's take the Cranbrook. Morey, you drive." He handed Morey the keys.

They piled in the Cranbrook. Morey backed out of the

garage, down the driveway, and into the street. He slipped the gearshift down three notches and surged forward with a burst of power. Harvey sat next to him, gripping the dashboard, trying not to appear overly nervous about someone else driving his car, but failing miserably.

"What a beauty this is," Morey said wistfully. "Wouldn't want to sell it, I suppose?"

"No. I'm giving it to my son. Gonna drive it up to Chicago one of these days, park it in his garage, get me a new pickup truck, and that'll be the end of the parades for me."

"You can carry the Sausage Queen in a pickup truck," Morey pointed out. "Wayne Fleming hauls his Little League team in the parade in his pickup truck."

"Sausage Queens aren't hauled," Harvey said. "They are escorted, and in a vehicle befitting their station in life."

They pulled up to the school, where the parade was organizing. Morey piloted the car through the crowd, around the floats and past the high-school band to the front, where Addie Lefter was waiting, resplendent in her Sausage Queen gown, sash, and crown.

Harvey leaped from the passenger's seat, hurried to her side, and ushered her to the Cranbrook, where she took her rightful place in the backseat.

"Let the parade begin," he cried, slipping into the passenger's seat. Morey goosed the accelerator, and the Cranbrook jumped forward.

"Steady, steady. This isn't a school bus," Harvey cautioned. "Four miles an hour and no faster. You don't want to outrun the band. Drop her down a gear."

They rolled up Washington Street, past Sam's house and Grant's Hardware. People lined the route, waving and cheering. What a glory it was. A red-headed Sausage Queen, so beautiful it made the old men weep, thinking back on the Sausage Queens of their youth. Oh, to be young.

Dale Hinshaw was standing in front of the Rexall holding a cardboard poster with the words *John 3:16* printed on it. They looped the corner at Kivett's Five and Dime and passed the Legal Grounds Coffee Shop. Deena and Dr. Pierce stood out front, arm in arm, her head resting on his shoulder; they were smiling contentedly, looking every bit the newlyweds.

The rest of the day passed in a blur. After the parade, everyone walked over to the meetinghouse, where the ladies of the Circle were waiting with hearts eager to serve the Lord through the ministry of chicken and noodles. Addie ladled out the first serving as Bob Miles snapped her picture for the *Herald*.

The Circle labored over the steam table through the afternoon, dishing out their heavenly concoctions. They never faltered, not once. When the last plate was served, Fern looked at the clicker in her hand. Seven hundred and eighty-three meals, she announced to the Circle. A record. Then her voice caught, and she burst into tears.

Sam and Barbara and their boys stayed past six o'clock, helping clean up, then walked home in the late summer evening underneath the canopy of maple trees that arched over the streets.

"What a day this has been," Sam said, as he slid his arm around Barbara and pulled her near.

"Yes, indeed," Barbara agreed, settling into his embrace.

"Gross," Levi said. "They're going to kiss."

"Right in front of God and everybody," Sam said, and kissed Barbara flush on the lips.

The boys groaned with disgust.

"I'm proud of you," Sam told Barbara.

"What for?"

"For not entering the Sausage Queen contest. It would have been a terrible embarrassment to the other girls when you got all the votes."

"You think?" Barbara asked, with a chuckle.

"I know," Sam said. "I know."

Eleven

A Long Stretch of Afternoon

The end of September found Asa Peacock in his barn, staring out at the rain, listening to the weatherman on the radio prophesy an even wetter October. Miniature rivers coursed through the fields, carrying the topsoil down to the creek. Much more of this and his land would belong to a farmer downstream. A northwest wind had blown for three days and was starting to lay the beans over. Asa was wishing he'd gone into the insurance business like his brother. Fifty-six years old and retired down in Florida, golfing every day without a worry in the world.

It was twelve o'clock and off in the distance he could hear the noon whistle from the fire station in town. Vinny would be serving ham and beans at the Coffee Cup. Ham and beans on

Monday, meat loaf on Tuesday, Wednesday was beef manhattan day, spaghetti on Thursday, and a fish sandwich on Friday if you were Catholic, a cheeseburger if you weren't.

He was on his own for lunch. Jessie had driven up to the city to visit her sister. He ran across the barnyard, hopscotching around the puddles, and into the mudroom, where he pulled his boots off. He surveyed the leftovers in the refrigerator and elected to go with ham and beans at the Coffee Cup.

It was a ten-minute drive. He drove slowly, observing the runoff in the ditches and stopping on the bridge over the White Lick Creek to watch the frothy torrent of water and mud. He went past the Hodges' farm. A combine was stuck in the mud up to its axles. Ellis would never live that down.

People have long memories in Harmony. Stanley Farlow blew up his truck twenty years ago and people talk about it as if it were yesterday. It happened in the fall, about this time of year. He'd doused a brush pile with gasoline, thrown a match on it, and hustled back to his truck. To his eternal regret, his truck became mired in the mud ten feet from the brush pile. The fire crept across the grass and began licking at the tires. It took him three minutes to run the half mile back to the barn for his tractor, an impressive time for an elderly gentleman wearing clodhoppers, though not impressive enough. They heard the explosion all the way to town.

Asa rolled down Main Street. The square was thick with farmers waiting for the front to pass. He had to park two blocks away, in the funeral home parking lot, then hoof it through the rain over to the Coffee Cup. He stepped through the door, shook off the rain, and looked around for a seat. There was only one open, next to Dale Hinshaw at the counter. A desperation seat. A seat that came with a price—a half hour of Dale Hinshaw questioning your commitment to the Lord and speculating about the imminent return of Jesus.

Asa studied the bulletin board, hoping someone would vacate a booth, but with the rain coming down, they were there for the long haul, so after a few minutes he took the seat next to Dale.

"Hey, Dale. How ya doin'?"

"Just thankin' the Lord to be alive."

So that's who we should blame, Asa thought.

Heather Darnell stopped in front of him, a glass of water and tableware in one hand, a paper place mat in the other, which she arranged neatly in front of him. Asa gazed at her discretely. Such a beauty. She smiled. Thirty-two beautiful teeth, not a cavity among them. Her hair was done in a French braid. Asa loved French braids.

"Hi, Mr. Peacock."

"Hello, Heather. How are you?"

"Just dandy. What can I get for you?"

He studied the menu at length, even though he knew what he wanted, a clever ruse to keep her in his vicinity.

"Hmm, how about ham and beans and a glass of sweet tea," he said, handing her the menu.

"You get two sides with that. What would you like?"

"Oh, I didn't know it came with any sides. Maybe I better see the menu again."

He had developed ordering into an art form.

He studied the menu once more, looking up every now and then to gaze at Heather, who was waiting patiently. She was so much nicer than Penny, Vinny's wife. With Penny, you were lucky to get a menu. Penny terrorized the customers into submission, bending them to her will. "What'll you want and make it snappy. I don't have all day. And don't be making a mess everywhere, or you'll clean it up. I'm not your personal slave."

"We have good coleslaw," Heather volunteered.

"Coleslaw it is, then, with a dish of pudding," Asa said, returning the menu with a flourish.

She hurried off to place his order. His eyes followed her. He inadvertently licked his lips.

"Matthew 5:28," Dale said, snapping Asa out of his reverie.

"What?"

"Matthew 5:28. Whosoever looketh on a woman to lust after her hath committed adultery with her already in his heart."

It was going to be a long lunch. He glanced around to see if a booth had come open. No such luck.

"So what are the doctors sayin' about your heart?" he asked Dale, changing the subject.

The one thing Dale liked even more than quoting Scripture was discussing his ailments. He took Asa on a verbal tour of his body, starting with his toes, which had lately been aching with all this rain, and concluding ten minutes later with his scalp, which itched something terrible after his wife had switched brands of shampoo.

"So," Dale said, summarizing his ailments, "with all these other problems, I just hope I live long enough to get a heart transplant."

"We all hope that," Asa said with a charity he didn't feel.

"I can't help but wonder what the Lord's kept me around for," Dale pondered aloud.

"There are many of us who wonder the same thing," Asa said.

"I tell you one thing," Dale said. "If the Lord sees me through this, I'm gonna start my Scripture eggs ministry up again."

Three years before, Dale had housed a dozen chickens in his basement, feeding them scraps of paper with Scripture verses printed on them, then distributing their eggs to people who in his estimation needed saving—mostly Catholics, Democrats, and Masons. Mercifully, the chickens soon died of a poultry disease and the town was temporarily spared from Dale's attempts to save them.

Fortunately, Heather appeared and placed Asa's food before him. "Ham and beans, coleslaw, one pudding, and a glass of sweet tea. Enjoy."

"Thank you, Heather."

She turned to Dale. "Can I get you anything else, Mr. Hinshaw?"

"No, that's about it."

Heather bustled off. Dale stood, stretched, extracted a five-dollar bill from his wallet, and laid it on the counter, an exorbitant tip for Dale, who customarily left a Bible tract. Vinny rang him up at the cash register, Dale shuffled out the door into the rain, and all over the Coffee Cup people relaxed. Penny cleared away his dishes, swiped a wet rag across the counter, and then picked up the five-dollar bill and studied it.

"That tightwad," she said rather heatedly. "He's got a lot of nerve."

"What'd he do now?" Asa asked.

She handed him the five-dollar bill, which wasn't a five-dollar bill at all. Though it appeared genuine on one side, on the other it read: *Disappointed? You won't be if you accept Jesus as your Savior.*

"Well, that's Dale for you," Asa said, handing it back.

"That right there is why I don't go to church," Penny said. "Here Heather is working hard, trying to make it on her own, and Dale pulls that kind of nonsense. The cheapskate." She called him a few more names that, though justified, were unsuitable for public places. Then she wadded up Dale's "tip" and flung it in the wastebasket.

She appeared to be launching into another tirade when the bell over the door tinkled and Ralph Hodge walked in. Ralph Hodge, who, while he'd lived in this town, was a pastor's dream, the man they had warned about from their pulpits, the "before" picture, a walking abomination. That God hadn't struck him dead was a puzzle to many. And yet in his depravity he served a purpose. No matter how bad things got, people could take comfort they hadn't fallen as far as he had. But now Ralph was sober and holding down a job, and the town was sorely in need of a new bad example.

Ralph sat on the stool Dale had vacated. Asa reached over and shook his hand. "Ralph, good to see you. How ya doin'? I heard you were back in town. How's the missus?"

"She's fine. Thanks for asking. How's Jessie?"

"Off to the city to visit her sister."

Asa was not much of a conversationalist. He tended to run out of gas after a few questions. "Some weather we're having, isn't it?"

Ralph nodded his head in agreement. "Sure is."

Asa stirred another teaspoon of sugar into his tea. "Yes, sure is some weather we're having."

Ralph leaned closer. "Say, Asa. You're pretty good friends with Ellis, aren't you?"

"Yeah, I'd say so. Why do you ask?"

"Oh, I was just wondering if he said anything to you about me."

"Nope," Asa said.

"I can't figure him out. About three weeks ago he and Amanda stopped by the tourist cabins where we're stayin' and invited us to dinner, so we went, and he stayed out in the barn the whole time. Came in for ten minutes to eat, then went right back out. Then I saw him the other day at the Five and Dime and he barely spoke to me. I just want a chance to make things right with him."

The last thing Asa Peacock wanted was to wade into the Hodge family fracas. "Maybe he was feeling puny. Lot of sickness going around, what with all this rain we've been having. It sure is some weather we're having, isn't it?" He drank the last bit of his iced tea, made one final pass at his bowl of ham and beans, wiped his mouth, then rose to leave. "Sure has been good seein' you, Ralph. Be sure to tell the little lady I said hey."

Ralph sat alone at the counter another hour, watching Vinny at the grill. It was his day off from the glove factory and Sandy was working at the Wal-Mart. The last thing he wanted was to sit in the tourist cabin, alone, smelling the mold and mildew, watching a soap opera.

After a while, the din faded as the lunch hour ended and people returned to their jobs. Vinny and Penny were in the back room washing dishes, while Heather wiped down the counters with bleach water and refilled the salt and pepper shakers. Ralph sipped his coffee and watched the rain slide down the front window like tears.

Maybe he should never have come back, he thought. Maybe he and Sandy should have stayed out in California and written Amanda a letter instead. But he'd wanted to prove to Ellis that he'd reformed, that he was good for something after all. And he'd wanted to apologize. So the prodigal son came home. But with his father dead, there was no one to welcome him back. No ring for his finger. No fatted calf. No party. Just an older brother keeping score.

He wanted to be mad at Ellis, but couldn't muster the bitterness. No one to blame but himself. *Step number four: Make a searching and fearless moral inventory of yourself.* No one had held the bottle to his lips.

He looked out at the rain again, then glanced at the clock over the grill. One thirty. Another three hours before Sandy got home. This was when he missed the liquor the most. The long stretch of afternoon with nothing to do and Sandy gone. The god-awful thirst, the temptation to crawl back in the bottle.

He'd been going to AA at the Quaker meetinghouse on Wednesday nights. He and Uly Grant and a handful of people he'd never met. Seven o'clock every Wednesday, sitting in folding chairs and talking about how much they missed it. The taste, the liquid warmth spreading through his body, calming, soothing. The rain pounded down harder, slanting against the window.

Two years and four months without a drink and not one bit easier.

He wondered if Uly was at the hardware store. Maybe he'd go visit him for a bit. He pulled a five-dollar bill from his wallet and laid it on the counter, then turned and walked from the Coffee Cup and into the rain. Past the Kroger and the Buckhorn, where he paused to stare in the window at the smear of colors from the neon beer signs along the back wall.

Most people remembered their first kiss. Ralph Hodge remembered his first beer. He was sixteen. The summer his father and Ellis had driven to Colorado, leaving him home to finish cutting the hay. The third day it had hit ninety-eight degrees. He'd quit the fields early and driven the farm truck into town, where he'd ended up going into the Buckhorn on a dare from some friends. One beer, then two, then three, then he'd lost count.

If he closed his eyes, he could still taste it.

He raked a trembly hand through his hair, pushing it up and back, then turned the corner and walked down the pot-holed, brick alleyway and stood underneath a metal awning at the back door of the Buckhorn, out of the rain. There was a wooden crate next to the door, which he pulled under the awning and then sat on.

Sometimes he wondered how his life would have turned out if he'd gone on the trip to Denver with Ellis and their dad. He hadn't been invited, but maybe if he had asked, they'd have taken him along and things would have turned out different. Just maybe.

He watched the rain puddle in opalescent swirls on the oil-stained bricks. Days like this he wondered how people who didn't drink made it through. The back door was wedged open. He could hear the clink of bottles and Willie Nelson's "Stardust."

Jesus hadn't finished the story. Ralph had looked it up himself.

He'd hoped the older brother eventually came around, but if he did, Jesus never said so.

He'd driven by Ellis's farm that morning, thinking, what with all the rain, Ellis might have time to talk. But he'd been busy trying to loosen his combine from the mud.

"Can't talk now," Ellis had told him. "Got work to do."

Ralph had offered his help, which Ellis declined.

Ralph had lingered to watch. Ellis revved the engine, rocking the combine back and forth in a failed effort to dislodge it. Stuck. Then he'd piled boards underneath the rear wheels to give them purchase, but they slid sideways off the boards back into the mud.

Just like me, Ralph thought, as he sat on the wooden crate in the alley behind the bar. Just like me. Stuck in the mud with the flames drawing closer, like Stanley Farlow years before. Why bother trying? And he rose to his feet and walked in the bar.

Twelve

From Bad to Worse

Ellis Hodge couldn't remember the last time he'd been so mad. He waded through the mud to the rear of his combine, drew back his foot and let loose with a well-placed kick at a tire, only to slip and land on his backside in the mucky mess. A gush of vile curse words erupted from his mouth. Ordinarily reverent, he'd sworn more in one day than he had his entire life, with an artistry and intensity that would impress a sailor.

His anger had been building since May, when he'd first seen Ralph at the diner in the city. Ever since, he'd had the most pleasant dreams in which he'd killed his brother and buried his body on a remote corner of the farm. It got so he hated hearing the alarm clock ring.

"Dadnabbit! This fricka-fracka, ricka-racka piece of goll-darned spit is gonna be the death of me!" he yelled, heaving himself out of the mud and whacking the rear of the combine with a board.

What made it worse was that Miriam had warned him not to combine, that the ground was too muddy and he'd get stuck. Thankfully she was working today, substitute teaching at the high school. As long as he got the combine unstuck by four o'clock, she'd never know. She isn't the type to say "I told you so" and rub it in, though she did have a self-satisfied smile that set him on edge.

Then his brother had stopped by. Of all the genetic possibilities his parents could have formed with their union, they'd produced a no-good, alcoholic child-deserter. With Miriam gone and not a soul in sight, Ellis had been sorely tempted to kill him then. Knock him on the head with a board and pitch him in the hole the combine had dug. The perfect crime.

He would have done it too. Except at the last moment, just before he'd grabbed the board, he'd noticed Ralph's car and couldn't think of how to hide it. He thought of driving it into the river, but the nearest one was thirty miles away and he'd have to walk home. There was never a river around when you needed one.

He worked all morning trying to dislodge the combine, to no avail. A little before two, he phoned Asa Peacock to see if he'd come with his new John Deere tractor, the one that had treads like a tank and could slog through anything. The phone rang six times before their answering machine picked up. It was Jessie's voice: "Sorry we missed your call. We're probably out in the fields. Leave your name, and we'll call you back just as soon as we can."

Ellis swore under his breath and banged the phone down. He stomped through the kitchen, flung the door open, and walked through the wet grass to his truck. Asa was probably in his barn. He'd have to drive over to the Peacocks' and search him out. A ten-minute drive, a half hour for Asa to come with his tractor, and another half hour to pull the combine free. They could just make it before Miriam got home. That's if his luck held, which would be a first.

It hadn't been a stellar day for any of the Hodge men. Back in town, Ralph Hodge was seated in the Buckhorn bar, a beer in front of him. He was sniffing it, savoring the aroma, enjoying the sensation of the cold mug cupped in his hands. Two years and four months without a drink. He lifted the glass to his lips and tilted it. The beer hit the back of his throat. It felt like an ember, as if he'd ingested a live coal. He spit it back into the mug.

A scene from his past flooded his mind. Amanda was eight years old and cooking supper for them. His wife was passed out on the couch, and he sat in his recliner, mean-drunk, bellowing for Amanda to bring him another beer. She hadn't moved quickly enough to suit him, and he'd cuffed her in the head.

When he'd begun attending church, he'd prayed for God to take that memory away, but God hadn't seemed inclined to heed his prayer. Hardly a day passed that Ralph didn't think of it. It dug at him, like a thorn in his flesh.

He pushed back from the bar.

"Aren't ya gonna finish your beer?" Myron Farlow, the bartender, asked.

"No thanks. Don't know what I was doing coming in here in the first place."

He walked through the front door and into the sunlight. The rain had stopped, and the clouds had broken up. The sun shone down in bright shafts, blinding him momentarily. His foot caught on the door jamb, and he stumbled onto the sidewalk.

He looked up just as Ellis drove past, slowly, staring at him, a look of sheer disgust on his face.

Of all the people in the world.

He began jogging down the sidewalk alongside Ellis, waving for him to stop. Ellis turned his head away and drove straight ahead, picking up speed. Ralph slowed to a walk in front of Grant's Hardware just as Uly walked out carrying an armload of rakes to arrange across the front of the store for his leaf-raking display.

"Hey, Ralph."

Ralph didn't answer. He sat down on the curb in front of the store, his head down, utterly dejected.

"What's wrong with you?"

"Just made the worst mistake of my life. The first time I go into a bar in over two years and my brother Ellis had to see me." He sagged with misery.

"You went in the Buckhorn?" Uly asked. "You could have come to me. You know I'm here for you."

"I only took a sip, and it tasted terrible. I spit it right out. Then I was so ashamed of myself, I left, and that's when Ellis saw me. Would you talk to him for me, maybe explain what happened?"

Uly thought for a moment. "No, I won't. You have to accept responsibility for yourself. Your drinking has caused the damage, and it's up to you to repair it."

"I know. I know." He rose to his feet.

"Where are you going now?" Uly asked.

"Anywhere but the Buckhorn."

"Attaboy, Ralph. I'll see you Wednesday night. You call me if you need to talk."

"Will do." He shook Uly's hand good-bye.

As for Ellis, he wasn't a bit surprised. Miriam had been after him to ease up on his brother, consider that maybe he had changed. But Ellis had known better. Once a drunk always a drunk. He couldn't wait to tell her.

He turned left at the school and made his way through the country to Asa's farm. Asa was out in the barn, just as he'd figured. Ellis swore him to secrecy before telling him about getting his combine stuck in the mud.

"And that's not the worst of it. I'm driving by the Buckhorn and who should stagger out but my supposedly sober brother. Probably in there drinking his lunch."

"That can't be," Asa said. "I ate lunch with him myself. Ham and beans at the Coffee Cup." His stomach gurgled in affirmation. Asa turned his head and let out a discreet belch. "Pardon me. Boy, those ham and beans tear me up. Like I was saying, Ralph was at the Coffee Cup not more than an hour ago, and he was sober."

"That can't be. I saw him stumbling out of the Buckhorn, drunker than a monkey."

Asa looked at Ellis, then spoke quietly. "I'm not saying you're lying, Ellis, but are you sure there isn't a reasonable explanation?"

"I know what I saw."

"Ellis, we've been friends a long time. And in all the time I've known you, you haven't liked your brother. Now I know he's had his problems, and Lord knows he's made some terrible mistakes. But the Ralph Hodge I saw at the Coffee Cup seemed to be a different man."

"People don't change just like that. Now if you're gonna help me, we have to get goin'."

Asa shook his head in frustration, then climbed in his tractor and followed Ellis back to his farm. Ellis skirted around the edge of town, his blinkers on, avoiding the school so Miriam wouldn't see them.

A half hour later, they had the combine pulled free of the

mud and parked in the equipment shed. Ellis's mood had vastly improved.

"Thank you, Asa. I owe you one."

"Happy to help, Ellis. Hope you get things worked out with your brother."

"Not sure that's possible, as long as he keeps drinkin'."

Asa bowed his head, drew a circle in the mud with the toe of his boot, then looked at Ellis. "Remember what Pastor Sam said last Sunday, that every saint has a past and every sinner has a future."

"What's your point?"

"My point is that you're starting to sound like Dale Hinshaw and you were never like that before. You need to give your brother a chance. And that's all I'm gonna say. You take care now, Ellis."

Asa climbed back on his tractor, fired it up, and headed east toward town. Ellis watched from his driveway, mystified how a smart man like Asa Peacock could be so easily taken in by a drunkard.

He turned and walked toward the house, then heard the crunch of gravel behind him as Miriam pulled in their driveway. Perfect timing, he thought. He stepped to the side as she drove past and parked near the barn next to the clothesline.

"Hey, honey. How was your day at school?"

"Fine. What'd you do today?"

"Oh, this and that. First one thing and then another."

He put his arm around her and guided her into the house before she noticed the trench in the field and inquired about it.

"I saw Ralph," she said.

"Oh?"

"Yes, he was walking home from town, so I gave him a ride. He wanted me to tell you something. Said you'd know what he was talking about."

"What's that?"

"He wanted me to tell you that things aren't always what they seem."

Ellis snorted.

"What did he mean by that?" Miriam asked.

"I saw him stagger out of the Buckhorn not an hour ago."

"Hmm, that's interesting. He certainly wasn't drunk when I spoke to him. Must have been your imagination. By the way, Amanda asked me this morning if they could come over for dinner this Friday, so I invited them. And I do not want you hiding out in the barn the whole time they're here."

The world had gone crazy.

He spent the rest of the day in the barn, seething. Then after supper he drove over to the tourist cabins, pulled up to number five, got out, and knocked on the door. Ralph answered on the second knock. He and Sandy were eating at a folding TV tray beside the bed. Ravioli from a can, cooked on a hot plate that sat atop a chest of drawers.

Ellis pulled his checkbook from his back pocket. "How much this time?"

"What do you mean?"

"Last time it cost me thirty thousand to make you leave. What'll it cost this time?"

Sandy walked over and stood beside Ralph. "We don't want your money. We came here to be near our family."

"Well, your family doesn't want you here, so why don't you just go back to California and we'll all be better off."

"I don't blame you for being mad at us," Ralph said. "I would be too, if I were you. But our daughter's here and we're staying."

Ellis scoffed. "Your daughter! Why didn't you think about your daughter when you were gettin' drunk every day and knockin' her around?"

Ralph straightened up. "I don't need you or anyone else to remind me how badly I've failed as a father. I think of that every day. Now I intend to do something about it, if Amanda will let me."

Ellis poked his finger in Ralph's chest. "Not here you won't, and not now. You stay away from her or, so help me God, I'll make your life miserable."

Ralph swept his hand around the room. "We cook on a hot plate and sleep on a broken-down mattress in a bug infested room, so we can pay you back the money you gave us. You keep our daughter from us and won't give us a second chance no matter how hard we try. Brother, how could you possibly make our life any more miserable than it already is?"

For a brief moment, Ellis was ashamed of himself. But the feeling passed quickly. "Don't bother comin' to dinner this Friday. You're not welcome in our home." Then he turned and left, spinning his truck wheels in the gravel in his haste to get away.

He didn't go straight home. He turned at Kivett's Five and Dime and drove past the meetinghouse, just as Sam was unlocking the door for a committee meeting. He thought of stopping and talking, then decided against it. Sam would urge him to forgive his brother. That was a pastor for you, always talking about love and forgiveness just when you wanted to punch someone in the nose.

He drove on, past Fern Hampton's house. She was raking the first batch of leaves into the gutter in a race against the setting sun. He coasted to a stop and leaned his head out the window.

"Hey, Fern."

"Ellis Hodge, I'm glad you stopped by. I have something to tell you." She thumped her rake on the sidewalk several times for emphasis. "Your brother is with that drunkards' group that meets in our church, and last Wednesday they didn't clean the coffeemaker after they were done with it. You tell him for me that if they don't start takin' a little better care of the kitchen, they'll have to find another place to meet."

"You might want to leave him a note, Fern. I'm not sure I'll be seeing him anytime soon."

She thumped her rake two more times. "I'll write him a letter, that's what I'll do. Send it registered mail. That way he can't deny gettin' it." She paused for a breath and another thump of her rake. "People like that, you try to help them and they don't appreciate it, they go back to their old ways. It's just like the Bible says, a dog returns to its vomit and a fool to his folly."

"It's been nice seein' you, Fern. You take care now." What a hard woman, he muttered under his breath as he drove away.

It is a curious phenomenon how the faults of another are glaring, while personal failings escape notice. And that was true for Ellis Hodge, who continued his drive toward home, utterly convinced his brother was still the bum he'd always been.

Thirteen
Patience

October passed in a flurry of activity. The farmers worked their fields, the distant rumble of combines could be heard through the day, and at night the drone of grain dryers lay over the land like a blanket. Dale Hinshaw was confined to home, his heart weakened after a frenzied burst of evangelism during which he'd distributed his fake five-dollar bills in restaurants across the county. Four weeks later, with not one convert to show for his efforts and a host of angry waitresses in his wake, he'd taken to his bed, a shell of his former self.

At Harmony Friends Meeting, Sam was compiling a file for Dale's funeral sermon, pleasant memories he could share with mourners in the event of Dale's demise. It was a piteously slender file, and Sam was trying to plump it up with quotes he'd culled from *Reader's Digest*.

"Why don't you just stand up there and tell the truth about him?" Frank the secretary suggested, standing in the doorway of Sam's office. "Let it be a lesson to others."

"That's not what eulogies are for," Sam pointed out. "Eulogies are for telling people how nice the deceased was even if you have to lie. Say, didn't Dale once lend you fifty cents for coffee?"

"Yes, he did."

"Good, I can mention that." He wrote on a Post-it Note and tucked it in Dale's file.

"But he charged me 25 percent interest each day," Frank said. "Ended up having to pay him back a dollar fifty-three."

Sam reached into his file and plucked out the note. "Probably I should leave the coffee story out," he said, wadding the note up and tossing it in the wastebasket in the corner. "Can you be sure to let me know if you hear any nice stories about Dale?"

"In the off chance that happens, you'll be the first to know," Frank promised, sauntering back to his office.

It was Friday, and Sam was mostly done with his sermon. He needed a closing illustration about patience. He'd been preaching a series on the fruits of the Spirit from the fifth chapter of Galatians: love, joy, peace, patience, kindness, goodness, faithfulness, gentleness, and self-control. The problem with living in Harmony most of his life was that he hadn't been exposed to many instances of patience. He had numerous stories about impatience, most of them involving his secretary.

"When are you gonna pick the hymns so I can do the bulletin for this Sunday?" Frank yelled from his office. "I want to get out of here sometime before midnight, for cryin' out loud."

"All Creatures of Our God and King," "'Tis So Sweet to Trust in Jesus," and "When We All Get to Heaven."

"What about the Scripture reading?" Frank yelled.

"Galatians 5:22–23. The fruits of the Spirit. Same as last week."

Sam could hear the clickety-clack of Frank's manual typewriter as he pecked in the numbers.

"It would be a whole lot easier to use the computer," Sam said. "You wouldn't have to retype everything all over again each week. Just plug in the numbers and print it out, easy as pie."

"Tell you what, Sam. If the hard drive in my Underwood ever crashes, I'll use that fancy computer of yours. Until then, I'll stick with this."

Why, Sam wondered to himself, did people fight change so when it came to the church? The irony of it. Dale Hinshaw going around railing against any and all theological enlightenment, wanting to drag the church back to the seventeenth century. But when it came to his health, he was willing to forego leeches and bloodletting and have a heart transplant. What was it about religion that made people so stuck in the mud? It made him mad just thinking about it.

"You could at least clean the gunk out of the letter e. It's start-ing to look like an o," he yelled in to Frank.

"Boy, for someone who's going to preach about patience, you sure are a grouch today," Frank yelled back.

Being in no mood to write about patience, Sam switched off his computer. To heck with a closing illustration, he thought. I'll just tell them to be patient if they know what's good for them.

Dale's deathwatch was wearing him down. For the past three days, convinced the angels were hovering about ready to carry him home, Dale had summoned Sam to his bedside. Sam flinched every time the phone rang. In his less charitable moments, he wished Dale would die and get it over with.

The next week was the boys' fall break from school. Sam and his family had planned for some time to visit Barbara's parents at their farm, two hours south. Given Dale's affinity for putting people out, he would likely die the night before they left and ruin Sam's one opportunity to get away.

For the past week, Dale had been propped up in a hospital bed in his living room next to his picture window, which he rapped on when anyone walked past. He would motion for them to come in, then apprise them of his suffering. Sam walked the long way home to avoid Dale's litany of woe.

All in all, it had been a gruesome week in ministry. Ralph and Sandy Hodge had been attending Harmony Friends the past two Sundays. Ellis had visited the office and asked Sam to kick them out.

"I can't do that," Sam had explained. "They've done nothing wrong."

"What do you mean they haven't done anything wrong? They're drunks and they abandoned their only child. That don't seem like good Christian behavior to me."

"Ellis, does Miriam know you're here?"

Ellis had studied the tops of his boots. "What's that got to do with anything?"

"I just wondered what she might think of your request to kick your brother out of church."

"She'd take my side."

"Well, Ellis, I'm sorry, but I can't," Sam had told him. "Jesus took in everyone and so must we."

"You asked Bob Miles's dad to leave that one time."

The problem with some people, Sam thought, is that they have too long a memory.

"That's because he was being abusive to other people. Ralph and Sandy have been perfectly cordial." He had paused, debating what to say next. He dreaded having to challenge people, but felt the time had come for some frank talk. "Ellis, it's no secret that you've been treating your brother shabbily. He came here wanting to make amends and heal relationships, and you've been most unkind to him. I'm asking you to make room in your heart for your brother. Not just for your brother's sake, but for Amanda's also. You're asking her to choose against her parents, and no one should do that to a child."

"Well, sometimes kids don't know what's best for them."

"That's true, but that isn't the case here. Amanda is a very capable young lady, wiser than many adults I know. Besides, you can't keep her away from her parents all her life."

"Well, I can't believe you'd take their side," Ellis had said, then had turned and walked from Sam's office.

Sam had phoned him the next day and left a message, but Ellis hadn't returned his call.

First, it had been Dale Hinshaw driving him nuts, then Ellis Hodge, and now Frank, his secretary. What is it with old men? Sam wondered. Do they take lessons on how to be crotchety? Dear Lord, don't let me get like that, he prayed.

He'd hoped a rousing sermon on patience would melt their hearts, though he wasn't overly optimistic. The problem with preaching sermons people needed to hear was that the people who needed most to hear them thought they were intended for someone else.

Lacking a personal illustration, Sam decided to finish the sermon with the parable of the lost sheep in Luke 15, though not without misgivings. When he'd preached on that text two years before, Asa Peacock had approached him after worship, wearing an uncharacteristic frown. "That shepherd shoulda quit while he was ahead. Sheep aren't worth the trouble."

Sam had tried to explain that the parable was actually about the patience of God and the worth of the individual, but Asa hadn't been persuaded. "Sheep are dumber than dirt. You could smack one upside the head and if it could talk, it'd ask you to do it again."

Biblical scholarship, Sam had decided long ago, didn't have much of a following in Harmony.

The next day was Saturday. He took his younger, Addison, to football practice in the morning, then spent the afternoon raking leaves. The angry whine of leaf blowers could be heard all over town. The week before, Bob Miles had written an editorial about noise pollution, calling down a host of plagues upon the inventor of the leaf blower, who, if God was just, was deep in the bowels of hell, without earplugs, a leaf blower screaming in his ear, driving him insane.

Sam was of the same mind and therefore able to resist Uly Grant's preachments about the superiority of the leaf blower. He bought four rakes instead, one for each member of the family. Saturday afternoon found him, Barbara, and their sons raking the leaves in a line across the yard and into the gutter for the street department to collect, saving back a pile for the boys to jump in and, when they wearied of raking, to burn in the driveway for the smell.

They worked four hours, then went in for supper—chili, peanut butter sandwiches, and iced tea. Sam's parents stopped by while they were washing dishes to compare leaf-raking notes. Sam's father is a purist. He prays over his rake, preparing for the task like a priest arranging the elements for Communion. He composts the leaves in a worm bed behind his barn, turning them once a week with a pitchfork, stirring coffee grounds into the mix each morning. Caffeine, he believes, energizes the worms, causing them to wiggle on the fishing hook, luring more fish.

He sells night crawlers each summer, on Friday evenings and Saturday mornings, to fishermen passing by on their way to Raccoon Lake two counties west. He posts a sign on the telephone pole at the corner of Main and Mulberry—*Home Grown Night Crawlers*—with an arrow pointing toward his home. He's been thinking of expanding into slugs and needs more leaves, so he asked Sam for his. They spread a painter's tarp on the street, raked the leaves onto it, then lifted them into the back of his father's pickup, and hauled them the four blocks to the Gardners' house on Mulberry Street.

"Yep, worms and slugs this year, and if that goes well, I might expand into crickets," Sam's father said. "There's big money in crickets."

"The sky's the limit," Sam said. "Today, earthworms. Tomorrow, you're the Rockefeller of the bait business."

His father smiled at the thought of it.

"So what's tomorrow's sermon about?" he asked Sam, raking the leaves out of the truck and onto the compost pile. This was an old scheme of Sam's father, who routinely asked him to divulge his sermon contents the day before church, so he wouldn't have to attend the next morning.

"I'm going to preach about a rich man who built larger and larger barns and laid up a big supply of bait, then decided to sit back and relax, and he died the next day. Maybe you oughta come hear it."

His father hitched up his pants, then studied him for a moment. "I thought you were preaching on the fruits of the Spirit."

Sam chuckled. "You got me there, Dad. Actually, I'm going to talk about patience."

"Fat lot of good that'll do."

"Well, it never hurts to try."

He raked another clump of leaves out of the truck. "Patience, huh? Well, your mother could certainly use that sermon. I'll recommend she pay close attention."

"Thanks, Dad."

Sam's father eased himself down off the tailgate, walked into the barn, flipped on the floodlights, and returned with a broom to sweep out the last of the leaves. "It'll be sweet romance all winter long and come spring, there'll be young 'uns poppin' out all over. Yessiree, money in the bank."

His annual discourse on worm propagation was the closest he'd ever come to talking with Sam about reproduction. As a child, Sam thought babies came from compost piles.

They closed the tailgate with a resounding thunk, then climbed in the cab of the truck and drove back to Sam's house. Piles of leaves lined the streets, like watchers of a parade. They drove this gauntlet of color, taking care not to drive too fast, lest leaves be scattered in their wake.

"Looks like winter's on the way," Sam's father said, anticipating the cold with a shiver.

"Any day now," Sam said, shifting from second gear to third in front of Bea Majors's home. "Why don't you take some of your worm money and go to Florida this year for a month or so?"

"What would your mother do?"

"I was thinking you'd take her with you," Sam said.

"Kinda takes all the fun out of it."

"You better not let her hear you say that, or you won't be in any kind of shape to go to Florida."

"Can't go to Florida anyway. Gotta stay here and watch my worms."

Uly Grant was standing in his driveway, burning leaves, the flames licking the edges of the piles, a glowing thread of light in the autumn dark. They turned the corner and drove past Dale Hinshaw's home.

"You know, if you were any kind of pastor, you'd rake Dale's leaves."

"It's my job to equip the church members for ministry," Sam said. "Why don't you rake them? That way we'll both be doing what we should."

"For a man of the cloth, you sure are sneaky."

"Got to be to keep up with my parishioners," Sam said.

They turned into his driveway and rolled to a stop in front of the garage, alongside the kitchen door. They sat in the truck, just the two of them, studying the yard, thinking their thoughts.

"Yep, gonna be some winter," Sam's father said after a bit. "If I didn't have so much to do, I wouldn't mind gettin' down to Florida. Don't see it happening, though."

"You think you got it bad. If Dale Hinshaw dies, I have to think up twenty minutes of nice things to say about him."

Sam's father winced. "I don't envy you that."

"You know something nice I could say about him?"

He thought for the longest time. "Nothing comes to mind."

"If something does, will you let me know?"

"You'll be the first to know," Sam's father promised. "Yessiree bob, the first to know."

fourteen

Out with the Old, In with the New

The phone call came the first day of November, on a Monday morning, Sam Gardner's day off. He'd just settled into his recliner to read the Sunday paper, which had arrived from the city in that morning's mail. He'd read the front section, then the comics, and then the advice columns, in that order. He surveyed the obituaries, to make sure no one he knew had died, and had just turned to the television section to preview that week's drivel when the telephone rang.

"Can you get that?" he yelled to Barbara. "I'm not home, so take a message."

He heard his wife pick up the phone in the next room.

"Sam, it's for you."

"Daggone it all, why can't you take a message?" he grumbled. "It's my day off."

"You need to take this one," Barbara said, handing him the telephone.

"Hello," he said, rather gruffly, in order to discourage a lengthy conversation.

"It's Dale," Dolores Hinshaw began.

Of course, it would be Dale, Sam thought. Who else but Dale Hinshaw would ruin my day off?

"The hospital called. They have a heart for him. We're supposed to be at the hospital in three hours. I'm too upset to drive and Dale can't and I called my sister but she's not home. Harvey Muldock said he'd take us, but he and Eunice went up to Chicago to see their son and all our kids are at work and we can't get hold of them and I don't know what we're gonna do. I called the hospital to ask if they could just keep it in Tupperware until we got there, but I guess they don't do that."

Then she let out a wail, which Barbara heard from across the room. Sam covered the telephone mouthpiece with his hand, turned, and smiled at his wife. "Honey, did you have any plans today?"

"Laundry, grocery shopping, housecleaning, taking the boys to the dentist after school, then to the barbershop for haircuts, then cooking supper and making cupcakes for Addison's class tomorrow. Other than that, my day's wide open. Tell you what though, if you want to do all that, I'll be happy to help the Hinshaws."

Sam grimaced. "Did you try Ellis Hodge?" he asked Dolores.

"He and Miriam are visiting her sister. Don't you remember? They asked for prayers for her yesterday in church. She's got thrombosis."

"I have an idea," he said, cursing his bad luck even as he spoke. "Why don't I come by and drive you and Dale to the hospital?"

"Oh, Sam, thank you. When can you be here?"

"Give me fifteen minutes."

"See you then."

He hung up the phone, his shoulders slumping, bowed in defeat. "There goes my day off."

"A day off. Boy, wouldn't that be nice."

So much for a sympathetic ear.

He tromped upstairs to brush his teeth, comb his hair, and change his shirt. Days like this, he wished he sold shoes. Eight to five, an hour for lunch, weekends off, no meetings at night, no disgruntled customers phoning his house to complain, plus a 50 percent discount on shoes. A sweet deal, if you could swing it.

His car was low on gas, so he stopped past Logan's Mobil to top it off. He drove over the rubber hose and could hear the bell sounding inside the garage. Though Logan's is full service, it is painfully slow. The sign out front says *Same Day Service,* which the uninitiated might think is a reference to engine repairs, but it isn't. That's how long it takes Nate Logan to scoot out from underneath a car, wash his hands, and make his way out to the pumps, where he eventually fills the tank, though not before complaining about his bad knees or various other maladies.

Sam had learned long ago not to ask Nate how he was unless he was prepared to spend the day listening.

For years, people have been pleading with Nate to make it a self-serve station, but he's resisted. Full service is his way of guaranteeing a captive audience. He sets the pump on the first notch and jabbers away for the fifteen minutes it takes to fill the tank. Only after the pump has shut off does he bother to check the oil and wash the windshield, maintaining a steady monologue all the while.

Sam was ten minutes late. By the time he arrived, Dale and Dolores were standing at the end of their driveway, suitcases in hand. Sam lifted their bags into the trunk, then opened the back door for them to get in.

"I better ride up front," Dale said. "Otherwise, I'll get carsick and throw up everywhere."

What a day this is going to be, Sam thought miserably.

They drove through town to Main Street, then headed east toward the interstate. Fifteen minutes later they were sandwiched between two semis, hurtling along at seventy miles an hour. Sam had a white-knuckled grip on the steering wheel while Dale yammered in his right ear.

"Sure hope those doctors are Christians," he said.

"What's their religion got to do with anything?" Sam asked. "There are plenty of wonderful surgeons who aren't Christian."

"I read in my *Mighty Men of God* magazine about this pastor in Alabama getting operated on and his doctors was Muslim and they found out he was a Christian while he was bein' operated on and they tried to kill him right there on the table and would have if one of the nurses hadn't been Christian and shot 'em dead. Thank the Lord for a God-fearing woman, that's all I can say."

"That's ridiculous, Dale. I never heard of that happening."

"And do you really think you would with the liberal press we have in this country?" He reached up and removed the large cross he customarily wore around his neck. "No use agitatin' them when they got a scalpel not six inches from my throat." He passed it back to Dolores. "Why don't you keep this in your purse until after my surgery. Don't want to wave a red flag in their faces."

They rode on in silence for a half hour. Sam was hesitant to speak, fearing it might give Dale a new topic and he'd be off to the races. Dolores would occasionally comment favorably about a passing barn or farmhouse, and Sam would nod his head agreeably. After a while, the hum of the road lulled the Hinshaws to sleep and Sam relaxed, almost enjoying the trip.

Thirty miles south of the city, Dale revived. He yawned and stretched, then rubbed his eyes. The farmland changed into suburbs, and the fields gave way to beige homes arrayed in domino lines.

"Sure hope I don't get a woman's heart," Dale said. He turned to Sam, "You think they'd do that to me?"

"I'm not sure, Dale. I don't know much about this kind of thing. But I'm sure if they give you a woman's heart, it'll be all right."

Dale harrumphed. "I was listening to Brother Eddie on his radio program and he was talking about organ transplants and he's not for them. Do you ever listen to him?"

Brother Eddie had a loose bolt above his neck and for years had plied the nighttime airwaves with his twaddle. Sam had listened to him in college for kicks. "Not for a long while," he answered Dale.

"Anyway, he was talking about this man who got a woman's heart and the next thing you know he'd turned into a homosexual and was wearing high heels and everything. Had a wife and three kids, was a deacon in his church, sang in the choir, and belonged to the Kiwanas. And he left all that to run off with some artist fella and now they wear dresses and sing in nightclubs. Brother Eddie had actually known the man." He shook his head at the depravity of it.

"Hasn't Brother Eddie also predicted the end of the world about a dozen times so far?"

"I don't know about that. Maybe once or twice," Dale conceded. "That don't mean he's wrong all the time."

Sam exited the interstate and turned onto a surface street that carried them to the hospital. He pulled up to the front entrance and deposited Dale and Dolores, then went to park his car. When he returned, he found Dale and Dolores standing near the registration desk. Dale was gawking at a crucifix mounted on the wall. He leaned over and whispered to Sam, "I didn't know this was a Catholic hospital."

"Why's that matter? It's a good hospital. One of the best in the nation for transplants."

"Hope they don't give me a Catholic heart, that's all. You know they put people under to operate on 'em and sneak in a priest to baptize 'em. They do the same thing if you're in an accident. You'll be layin' in the street with a car on top of you and a priest is praying over you and the next thing you know you're sayin' the rosary and eatin' fish on Fridays. Promise you won't let 'em baptize me, Sam."

People were beginning to stare at them, frowning.

"Sure, Dale, I promise."

Fortunately, a nurse appeared and whisked Dale away to prepare him for the surgery. It was nearing lunchtime, so Sam and Dolores went to the cafeteria to begin their long wait. It was crowded with doctors and nurses, but they found a small table in one corner. Dolores nibbled the edges of her hamburger, clearly distracted. "You do think he'll make it, don't you, Sam?"

Sam reached across the table and patted her hand. "He's going to be fine."

The intercom over their heads sputtered to life. "Could Dolores Hinshaw please come to the surgery waiting room. Dolores Hinshaw, to the surgery waiting room."

"Oh my Lord, he's dead already," she cried, leaping to her feet.

To his shame, Sam's first thought was that with Dale dead, he wouldn't have to spend his whole day at the hospital after all. Then his pastoral instincts kicked in, and he hurried out of the cafeteria and down the hallway after Dolores.

"What's wrong with my husband?" Dolores asked the woman behind the waiting-room desk.

"The doctor will be out with you in a moment, ma'am. Why don't you have a seat."

Sam steered Dolores to a chair, then sat beside her. He glanced around the waiting room, studying the people, most of whom were staring slack-jawed at the television.

Thirty minutes and two magazines later, a doctor emerged and caught Dolores's eye.

"Mrs. Hinshaw?"

"Yes, that's me."

"Just wanted to let you know we're starting things up." He outlined the procedure, trying to put Dolores at ease, and then turned to Sam. "Are you their son?"

Heaven forbid, Sam thought. "Sam Gardner," he said, extending his hand. "I'm the Hinshaws' pastor."

"Oh, I see. Yes, I had the impression Mr. Hinshaw was deeply religious."

You don't know the half of it, Sam thought.

"He kept asking me if I was saved. I told him I was Episcopalian."

"Very interesting," Sam said.

"Probably the anesthesia," the doctor guessed. "Sometimes it makes people say funny things."

"That must have been it," Sam agreed hastily.

"Well, I just wanted to touch base with the family before we did the surgery."

"How long will it take?" Dolores asked.

"Depends on what we find when we get in there, but probably no more than six hours. So why don't you relax, maybe get a bite to eat. We'll send someone out every hour or so to let you know how things are going."

He gave Dolores an Episcopalian hug—modest but heartfelt—then excused himself.

Sam steered Dolores to a quiet corner, away from the television, and sat beside her. An hour passed. They'd worked the crossword puzzle and the word search and had settled in for a long wait, when a flurry of activity by the registration desk caught their attention.

"There they are," Asa Peacock said, pointing at Sam and Dolores.

It appeared half the town had come: Asa's wife, Jessie; Dale's barber, Kyle Weathers; Bea and Opal Majors; Oscar and Livinia Purdy from the Dairy Queen; Mabel Morrison and the lovely Deena Morrison; Vinny and Penny from the Coffee Cup; Bob Miles from the *Herald*; Frank the secretary; Morey Lefter; Hester Gladden; Stanley Farlow; Fern Hampton; and Judy Iverson and her Chinese twins. At the back of the bunch, looking awkwardly about, stood Ralph and Sandy Hodge.

Dolores, clearly moved, began to weep. "I can't believe you're all here."

"First heart transplant in Harmony," Bob Miles said, settling into a chair beside Sam. "Wouldn't have missed it for the world. Say, you think they'd let me in to take a few pictures?"

"Barbara wanted to come, but she couldn't find a babysitter," Frank told Sam. "She's the one who called everybody. We got the chain of prayer going." He turned to face Dolores. "How you holding up?"

"The Baptists loaned us their bus. Morey drove us," Asa said. "They're praying for you too."

"All the churches are," Frank said. "I called 'em all. Called the Quaker superintendent too. They're e-mailing all the meetings."

Sam sat in his chair, utterly dazed, verging on tears. What wonderful, beautiful people, he thought. They make me so crazy, I could scream sometimes, and then they go and do something like this. Dear Lord, thank You for each and every one of them. Make me more like them.

"Anybody care for a Dilly Bar?" Oscar Purdy asked. "Brought a whole cooler of them."

And so the afternoon passed. Twenty-four Harmonians, gathered in a circle, nibbling on Dilly Bars, fussing over Dolores, entertained by the Chinese twins, who turned somersaults to spirited applause, then occasionally falling silent to pray for a man whose recovery they would likely one day regret, but whom their Christian faith called them to love nonetheless.

fifteen

A Serving of Guilt

The Monday before Thanksgiving found Sam Gardner at home, resting in his easy chair, surveying that week's edition of the *Herald*.

"Did you know that pound for pound, hamburger costs more than a new car?" he asked Barbara.

"I had no idea. Who told you that?"

"It says so right here in the *Herald*. And brown sugar won't harden if you store it in the freezer."

"You're a fount of information," Barbara said.

Sam turned the page to the "Twenty-five Years Ago This Week" column. "Looks like I made the newspaper."

"What did you do now?"

Sam read aloud, "Sam Gardner, the son of Charles and Gloria Gardner, was the recipient of the Ora Crandell Memorial Scholarship. He will receive a fifty-dollar scholarship to the college of his choice and a shoe-care kit, compliments of Morrison's Menswear."

"Do you still have it?" Barbara asked.

"The shoe-care kit?"

"No, the fifty dollars."

"Spent it a long time ago," Sam reported.

"Rats. I wanted to eat out tonight."

"Looks like you're out of luck." He turned the page and scanned the church news. "Unless you want to eat with the Methodists in Cartersburg. They're holding an early Thanksgiving dinner tonight for the poor. Want to go?"

"We probably don't qualify," Barbara pointed out.

"We could wear old clothes. They'd never guess."

"You are a sick man, Sam Gardner."

"Nope, just hungry. What's for lunch?"

"Baloney sandwiches and Cheetos?"

"Sounds good to me. You fix it, and I'll do the dishes."

"You're on," Barbara agreed.

Sam lived for Mondays. The kids were in school, their phone was off the hook, and Frank the secretary was under strict instructions not to disturb him unless someone died. The afternoon stretched before him, an unpainted canvas of relaxation.

"Want to go for a walk after lunch?" Barbara asked.

"Sure."

They left the house after lunch, heading south past the school and the Co-op and out into the country. The leaves had fallen and it was a bright, crisp day. The crops had been harvested, and cornstalks lay wounded in a field, cut off at the knees.

A pickup truck lurched into view and rolled to a stop beside them. Ellis Hodge rolled down his window. "Hey, Sam. Hey, Barbara. Need a ride?"

"No, thank you. We're just out for a little fresh air," Sam explained. "How's Ellis doing?"

"If I was any better, I'd be twins. Got the crops in and heading into town to give the bank all my money. Say, I saw you mentioned in the newspaper, Sam. I'd forgotten all about you winning the Ora Crandell award."

"My claim to fame."

"How's the family?" Barbara asked.

"We're all doing fine."

"How about Ralph and Sandy? How are they?"

Sam gave Barbara a discreet kick in the ankle. She was wandering into dangerous territory. Probably on purpose, knowing her. Ellis's obstinacy regarding his brother annoyed her to no end.

"Still alive, I reckon," Ellis said rather grumpily.

"It must be nice to have a brother," Barbara continued, seemingly oblivious to Ellis's discomfort. "I always wanted a brother, but never had one."

"You can have mine," Ellis offered.

"Ellis Hodge, you ought to be ashamed of—"

"Ellis, you have a nice day," Sam interrupted, nudging Barbara along. "We need to finish our walk. Give Miriam and Amanda our best."

Ellis assured them he would, then accelerated away toward town.

"Would you stop picking on that poor man," Sam said. "Every time you see him, you ask about his brother. Has it ever occurred to you that he might not want to talk about it?"

"I just thought that, since you won't encourage him to forgive his brother, I would."

"It's not that simple," Sam said. "You can't compel someone to forgive someone else. And try seeing it from Ellis's perspective. If Ralph had neglected our sons, would you be eager to forgive him?"

Barbara didn't answer.

"He just needs time," Sam said. "Ellis is a good guy. He'll come around."

They walked another mile, to the edge of Stanley Farlow's old farm, before turning around and heading back home. Barbara was a little peeved, Sam could tell. After a while, the water tower came into view.

"Have I ever told you how my grandparents met?" Sam asked.

"About a million times."

Sam chuckled. By now they were at the edge of town, walking past the cemetery on the hill above the school. "I wonder what's harder," Sam mused. "Whether it's harder to change or to make people believe you've changed."

"Probably it's harder to get people to believe you've changed."

"That would certainly explain Ellis's attitude," Sam said.

"You know, a guy like Ralph doesn't stand a chance. He's been an alcoholic for so many years no one can believe he's different. I wouldn't be surprised if he started drinking again."

Sam thought for a moment. "It must be tough being Ralph Hodge. Ever since they've come back, I've been wondering what I would say to him if he came to me for advice. My life has been so easy, I'm not sure what I could say that wouldn't sound like a mindless platitude."

They passed the school just as the bell rang and the kids flooded out the front doors. They spied their sons amid the surging mob and called out their names. Addison, still too young to be embarrassed by his parents, came running toward them. Levi, their older one, was clearly mortified at his mother and father's presence. In front of his friends, no less.

"We're over here, honey," Barbara called out, waving.

His friends snickered. Levi frowned, turned, and began walking in the other direction.

"I don't think he likes being called honey," Sam observed.

Barbara sighed.

"Look on the bright side," Sam said. "They'll be going off to college before we know it, and we can sleep in and not have to drink from jelly glasses."

"Or open the refrigerator and find that someone put an empty milk carton back in," Barbara added.

"Or find wet bath towels underneath their beds."

"Don't forget sticky doorknobs and potato chips between the couch cushions."

"So will we travel the world and learn how to cook exotic dishes and read all the books we were supposed to have read in college?" Barbara asked.

"Probably not," Sam said. "But I'll take you to the Masonic Lodge fish fry if you want and we can read the *Herald*."

"I guess that'll have to do," Barbara said, taking his arm.

Addison squirmed his way in between them. His face was a study of dried milk and faint red tomato sauce.

"Let me guess, you had spaghetti for lunch," Sam said.

"Yep, and chocolate milk."

"Sounds delicious," Sam said. "Nothing like spaghetti and chocolate milk to perk a man up."

They'd not been home long when Asa Peacock pulled in their driveway with a load of firewood, which the boys stacked in a lopsided row behind the garage, while Barbara made supper and Sam went to visit Dale, who had been cut loose from the hospital the week before and sent home to recuperate.

Persuaded God had spared his life for some noble purpose, Dale had been agitating Sam to reconsider canceling the revival so they could bring in an evangelist he'd seen on television—a man who'd been a missionary in Africa, where the cannibals ate his right leg before he could escape. Undeterred, he'd carved himself a new, albeit shorter, leg and now traveled the country enlightening the multitudes. Brother Lester, the One-Legged Evangelist. Like most folks of his theological persuasion, he leaned toward the right.

Sam had hoped the heart transplant would improve Dale's personality, though that hasn't happened. His new heart appears to be every bit as hard and unyielding as his previous one. When Sam had expressed reservations about Brother Lester visiting their church, Dale had blasted away at him. "Well, I can't say I'm surprised. Stanley Farlow told me that the whole time I was gone you didn't preach the Word once. Said you were nothing but a lukewarm ear tickler, and I'd have to say he's right."

Sam had been reading a book on the power of forgiveness. Written by a Catholic monk, it described in poetic language the benefits of pardon and mercy. Though Sam suspected the monk had never met anyone like Dale, he was still theoretically committed to the notion of turning the other cheek, so he went to visit Dale on his day off, in hopes of spreading some Christian cheer.

He didn't stay long. They discussed their Thanksgiving plans. Dale hinted around that a true minister of the gospel would invite lonely parishioners to Thanksgiving dinner at his house. "Yeah, we're just gonna be here by ourselves on Thanksgiving. The kids aren't coming in until Saturday. It'll just be me and the missus here by ourselves. Just the two of us. All alone. Here by ourselves."

"Saturday will be here before you know it," Sam said, determined not to host Dale Hinshaw yet another Thanksgiving.

"It might be my last Thanksgiving," Dale said mournfully. "That is, if I live that long. 'Course that's not my decision. But if the good Lord calls me home, I'll not complain. His will, not mine, be done."

Sam sat quietly, trying to imagine why God might want Dale in closer proximity.

"Well, you be sure to enjoy your family this Saturday," Sam said, rising to leave. "Tell your kids I said hello."

"Would you say a little prayer for us before you go? Maybe ask the Lord's blessing on us in our loneliness?"

Sam almost caved in, but managed to steel himself, pray a brief prayer, and escape before Dale Hinshaw ended up seated across from him at the Thanksgiving table, hogging the drumsticks.

He made it halfway home, before he was overcome with guilt and went back to invite the Hinshaws to Thanksgiving. "We'll be eating around noon."

He didn't mention it to Barbara until his parents arrived a little before eleven on Thanksgiving morning. "By the way, honey, I think Dale and Dolores might stop by for a little bite to eat. I seem to remember them saying they might. We might want to set a couple more places."

Sam's timing was exquisite. Just as she began to object, their front door opened and there stood his brother, Roger, and his latest girlfriend, Sabrina. Coming up the sidewalk behind them were the Hinshaws, clutching on to one another.

"Well, isn't this a nice surprise," Sam said. "Look, honey, Dale and Dolores are here. Come in, come in."

As it turned out, Dale wasn't able to squeeze a word in edgewise. Sabrina spent the entire dinner bemoaning global warming and lamenting the invention of the internal combustion engine.

Roger looked on, beaming at his girlfriend. "She's from San Francisco originally. She lived in a redwood tree for three weeks so it wouldn't be cut down. It was in all the newspapers."

Barbara and Sam smiled, contemplating the appropriate response to Roger's revelation.

"I'm looking forward to the dessert you brought," Barbara said. "It looks delicious. What exactly is it?"

"It's homemade yogurt," Roger said. "Sabrina made it from goat milk."

Roger doesn't date women; he dates causes, none of which last. By the next Thanksgiving, there'd be another girlfriend, probably someone from New York City who wrote poetry and belonged to a vegetable cooperative. But then Sam's mother asked Sabrina how she felt about children, which led to a lecture on overpopulation and the general irresponsibility of bringing someone into a world on the edge of collapse.

"That's why we got to go out and get people right with the Lord before the Rapture," Dale interjected, launching into a commercial for Brother Lester, who, despite losing a leg to cannibals, was still faithfully preaching the Word.

"It serves him for right for imposing his values on other cultures," said Sabrina, who then groaned about Western imperialism and religious colonialism.

Roger watched, glowing, as Sabrina prattled on, and when he kissed his mother good-bye, he whispered in her ear that he was thinking of proposing.

It was all his mother talked about while she and Sam and Barbara washed dishes. "Why can't they just live together?" she moaned.

It is a shock to hear a mother urge her offspring to shack up, but then an afternoon with Sabrina had a way of shattering time-honored values.

"Your poor mother," Barbara said that night, while she and Sam were lying in bed. "I bet she worries about Roger."

"At least she has me," Sam pointed out. "The winner of the Ora Crandell Memorial Scholarship. That ought to be enough glory for any mother."

"And you wear your accomplishments so lightly. Winning fifty dollars and a shoe-shine kit would make the average man insufferable, but you're the same humble man you've always been."

"I am, aren't I," Sam agreed.

They lay quietly in the dark as an occasional passing car cast shadows against their bedroom wall. Barbara was thinking of all the things she had to do the next day, and Sam was reaching back in his memory twenty-five years, when the world was his oyster and pearls seemed plenty.

Sixteen
The Man in the Window

ob Miles watched from across the street as Ned Kivett removed the Thanksgiving mannequins from his display window at the Five and Dime. Like most of the Five and Dime decorations, these had come with the store in 1956, when Ned had won the store from Marvin Danner in a poker game at the Odd Fellows Lodge. A thousand dollars in the hole, Marvin had offered Ned title to the Five and Dime instead. It had taken Ned less than a week to realize Marvin had gotten the better end of the stick.

In the window, Mr. and Mrs. Pilgrim were smiling happily at an Indian sporting a Mohawk haircut. The Indian was frowning, as if sensing he were about to get the shaft. He looked a little like Ned Kivett had in 1963.

Ned piled the mannequins in a shopping cart and pushed them through the store to the back room. Arms and legs hung lifelessly over the sides of the cart, casualties on their way to a storeroom burial. Ned stacked them in the corner next to the Easter Bunny, then loaded the Christmas decorations onto the cart and wheeled them to the front of the store. Another trip back to the storeroom for a load of snow—a bag of cotton that over the years had grayed to a wintry slush. Rudolph the reindeer, his red nose rubbed raw from years of children picking at it, stood next to Santa, who looked like an Odd Fellow after a hard night of fellowship.

Santa was actually Mr. Pilgrim in more festive garb. Ned had stripped him in the storeroom, wheeled him naked through the store, then propped him in the window before dressing him as Santa. He'd forgotten the extra padding and had returned to the storeroom in search of a pillow.

What a sorry mess, Bob thought, looking on from the sidewalk as Santa Claus mooned the passing traffic. He thought of taking a picture of that for the front page, but could just imagine the letters to the editor he'd receive.

You cannot imagine the disgust I felt when I opened your newspaper only to find a naked man staring back! These must surely be the last days the Bible warns about, when depravity of all sort is unfolding before our very eyes!

The year before, Bob Miles had written an editorial bemoaning the wretched state of the town's Christmas decorations—

three strands of lights, a half dozen plywood cutouts Wilbur Matthews made in his garage back in the '70s, and Ned Kivett's pathetic excuse for a Christmas display—to no avail.

Bob had even sponsored a Christmas decorating contest, to be judged by the Sausage Queen and other dignitaries, but no one had entered. First prize had been a year's subscription to the *Herald,* which was not much of an inducement since it was already free. Then he'd thought of sponsoring a beauty contest, a Miss North Pole, but his wife had nipped that in the bud.

Ellis and Amanda Hodge rumbled past in Ellis's truck. Amanda was driving, squinting through the windshield, appearing to be in sore need of corrective eyewear. It was remarkable, Bob thought to himself, how a girl who'd won the National Spelling Bee could be such a dreadful driver. Success had attached itself so firmly to Amanda, it was a jolt to witness her deficiencies behind the wheel.

A clap of crunching metal snapped him out of his ruminations and he looked up to see the Hodges' truck wrapped around a streetlamp. Though not a religious man, Bob breathed a prayer of thanksgiving for what would surely be a front-page photograph and hurried across the street, his camera at the ready.

Ellis had pulled a bandana from his pocket and was preparing to wipe away a slight stream of blood trickling from his nose.

"Not yet," Bob cried out, clicking away with his camera. "Let me get a shot of that blood!"

There was nothing like gore and mayhem to increase circulation.

Amanda reclined in the seat, unharmed, but dazed.

A small crowd began to gather around the truck, shouting advice.

"Get 'em out of that truck before it catches fire."

"Don't move them. They might have broken necks."

"Keep away from that blood! No telling what diseases he might have."

Ellis and Amanda scrunched down lower in the seat, thoroughly embarrassed.

"Somebody call an ambulance!"

Antifreeze leaked from the radiator onto the street.

"My Lord, that's gasoline," a voice yelled out. "She's gonna blow."

What a picture that would be, Bob thought. He studied the growing puddle. "It's just antifreeze," he reported, clearly disappointed.

Sam Gardner, sitting in the chair at Kyle's barbershop, had witnessed the entire calamity. He'd rushed from the shop and begun helping Amanda from the car. "Did the same thing myself when I was your age," he said, in an effort to console her. "Except I hit a Corvette." He pulled a handkerchief from his pocket and handed it to her. "Thank God for seat belts. You don't look any worse for the wear. Don't you worry about the truck. It can be replaced. You can't."

Ellis had climbed from the truck and was inspecting the front end of his once unblemished truck. Johnny Mackey rolled up in his ambulance, his siren fading into silence. He studied Ellis's nose. "Maybe we oughta take you to the hospital. I read this story once about a man who broke his nose and he didn't have it looked at and a bone splinter had poked itself into the brain and three days later the guy dropped over dead, just like that."

"I'm fine," Ellis grumbled.

Johnny pulled him aside. "You know, Ellis, events like this remind us of life's uncertainties. Why don't you and Miriam stop by tomorrow so we can discuss funeral prearrangements? We've got a special this week. A 10 percent discount on embalming with the purchase of every casket." He slipped Ellis a business card. "We never know when the Lord might call us home," he said with the solemnity befitting a mortician.

The crowd began to disperse, except for the men who lingered to offer counsel on how best to remove a truck from around a streetlamp. Ten minutes later, Nate Logan arrived with his tow truck, hitched it to the back of Ellis's truck, and pulled it loose with a long, loud screech, like fingernails on a chalkboard.

By then, Harvey Muldock, having caught wind of a potential customer, had appeared. "Got a real good deal on new trucks, Ellis. Why don't you and the little lady come on down and we'll fix you right up?"

"Vultures!" Ellis yelled, uncharacteristically for him. "You're all trying pick my carcass clean. Johnny Mackey wants to sell me a casket and now you're after me to buy a truck."

"Leave the man alone," Bob Miles ordered. "Can't you see he's in a state of shock." He put his arm around Ellis. "Now why don't you and Amanda lay down here on the street beside your truck and I'll get one last picture for the *Herald*."

This is all my brother's fault, Ellis fumed to himself. Not one good thing has happened since he moved back here.

Sam Gardner gave them a ride home. By then, half a dozen concerned citizens had phoned Miriam to tell her the news. The wreck grew in severity with each call. By the sixth one, Ellis and Amanda, or what was left of them, were being helicoptered to the hospital in the city, clinging to life, vestiges of their former selves.

Miriam was backing the car from the barn when they pulled in the driveway. She was so relieved they were alive, the destruction of the truck didn't faze her. "I thought you were dead. Oh my Lord, I thought you were gone." She began to weep, clutching Ellis and Amanda to her.

"It's my fault," Amanda said. "There was a naked man in Kivett's window and I was watching him."

Miriam reddened, and Ellis blushed.

"It wasn't Ned, was it?" Ellis asked. Rumors of Ned and his mannequins had been circulating for years.

"I couldn't tell. I couldn't see very well. I just saw his backside."

"Man ought to be arrested, standing naked in broad daylight like that," Ellis groused. "What's this world coming to?"

Losing his truck had soured him considerably.

It was suppertime. Miriam made Amanda's favorite meal—blueberry pancakes, milk, and bacon on the side. Then Amanda did her homework and went to bed, done in by the day's events.

Miriam and Ellis lingered at the supper table, contemplating life without a truck.

"It's that brother of mine," Ellis said. "He moves back and everything goes wrong. I tell you, Miriam, we ought to pack our bags and take Amanda and move out of this place. Not tell a soul in the world where we're going."

Miriam reached across the table and took his hand. "Ellis, you know you don't mean that. This is our home. And today wasn't your brother's fault. He wasn't anywhere around when you wrecked. You've had a rough day. Why don't you take a shower and let's go to bed."

Ellis hung his head, the picture of gloom. "Now that Amanda's seen a naked man, I suppose you'll have to give her the birds and the bees talk."

"Me? Why me? I thought we'd both do that . . ."

"You can't be serious. I'm a man. I can't be talking with her about those things. That's a mother's job. If she were a boy, it'd be different."

"I wonder if they told her anything in school."

"Not anymore. Dale Hinshaw made them stop. Remember?"

"Then let's have Dale talk to her," Miriam suggested.

"It would serve him right," Ellis agreed. "But let's not do that to Amanda."

They sighed.

"I'll talk to her this weekend," Miriam said. "Why don't you make yourself scarce Saturday morning and we'll have a girl talk then."

"I suppose I could go look for a new truck," he said with a sigh.

Upstairs, Amanda was listening through the heating duct, absolutely horrified. In a life that had seen bleak days, today was one of the worst. Not only had she wrecked Ellis's truck, Miriam was going to talk with her about sex. She thought of running away before Saturday morning. She imagined their conversation. Her listening and trying not to be embarrassed and thanking Miriam for telling her things she already knew, having heard all about sex from Melissa Yoder, her best friend. Not that Melissa was speaking from personal experience; she read widely.

Boys, Amanda thought, who needs them anyway? She'd seen her first naked man today and it was no big thrill. He'd been standing there in Kivett's window like a moron—pale, slack-jawed, and lifeless.

She lay in bed, estimating the number of days she had before going away to college.

Downstairs, the phone rang. She could hear Miriam speaking. "Hello, Ralph. Yes, she and Ellis were in a wreck, but they're all right. She's upstairs in bed just now. Would you and Sandy like to come by tomorrow to see her. I'm sure she'd love to see you."

Oh, great, Amanda thought, they'll come out, Ellis will go to the barn and sulk, and when he comes back in, he and Miriam will argue.

Lately, all they'd done was argue—Miriam reasoning with him, encouraging him to forgive his brother; Ellis standing firm against these graces, hidebound in his loathing.

It wasn't like she could talk to Ellis about it. She felt she had to be constantly grateful to Miriam and Ellis for taking her in five years ago when her real parents were drunkards. And though she appreciated their sacrifice, she felt their charity required her unwavering thankfulness. Melissa Yoder would occasionally talk back to her parents, the prerogative of every hormone-addled teenager. Amanda couldn't imagine doing that to Ellis and Miriam, after everything they had done for her. Now she'd wrecked their truck and the burden of gratitude weighed even heavier.

No way she could ever put them in a nursing home now. She'd go to college, they'd make sure of that, but then she would have to come back and take care of them in their dotage, wiping their drool and laundering their undershorts.

Amanda rolled to her side and thought of Ralph and Sandy, her real parents. As bad as they had been to her, she wished them well. How weird is that? she thought. I get mad at the people who helped me, but aren't angry at the people who would have ruined me. Then she felt even worse for thinking ill of Miriam and Ellis.

She knew he didn't do it on purpose, but sometimes Ellis made her feel she had to choose between them and her parents, like it was a contest with her affection as the prize.

For seventeen years old, Amanda Hodge was unusually per-
ceptive, but some things she'd never understand, like why Ellis
couldn't believe his brother had changed.

A few weeks before, she'd seen her parents at the Kroger.
They'd stood in the produce aisle, visiting. Her parents had been
looking at a two-bedroom house next to the school. "Maybe we
can work things out so we could spend more time together, like
regular families," her parents had told her. "We can start over."

She hadn't mentioned it to Miriam and Ellis. Not yet. She'd
thought about starting small, maybe living with them on the
weekends. She suspected Miriam wouldn't mind. Ellis, on
the other hand, would achieve orbit. She'd been ready to ask him
right before she'd hit the streetlamp and would have if not for
that naked man in Ned Kivett's window.

She watched out the window as snow began to spit against
the windowpane, wondering why it was some folks, once they
made up their minds about someone else, could never believe
something good about them. And there in the darkness, she
began to pray God would soften Ellis's heart, so it wouldn't break
the day she went home.

Seventeen

Home for the Holidays

It was two days before Christmas, and Dale Hinshaw was in his element. In a fit of Yuletide nostalgia and powered by a new heart, Dale had resurrected the progressive Nativity scene. It had been two years since the church's last progressive Nativity scene, and they hadn't had time to rehearse, which made it's flawless production all the more miraculous. "I tell you, the Lord's just got His hands all over this one. You can just feel Him here," he'd said to Sam while they were setting up the manger in Harvey Muldock's front yard.

Dr. Pierce and Deena Morrison were the blessed couple, Joseph and Mary, standing in Fern Hampton's driveway beside her privet hedge, looking both elated and fittingly sober after birthing the Messiah. As for Jesus, he was borrowed from the Baptist church, it being a barren year for the Quakers. Nine months old, the infant was performing in his second pageant, and he had risen to the occasion, wrapped in swaddling clothes and reposing in Harvey's front yard. Harvey's beloved Cranbrook convertible was parked alongside the manger, sporting a festive string of blinking Christmas lights along its bumpers.

The heavenly hosts—Miriam and Ellis Hodge and Stanley Farlow—were praising God in front of the Harmony Friends meetinghouse, while the shepherds—the youth group in bathrobes—were abiding in the empty lot next to Opal Majors's house.

It took twenty minutes to navigate the progressive Nativity route, with cookies and hot chocolate awaiting the weary pilgrims at Sam Gardner's home, which he'd offered before consulting his wife, who was at that very moment cleaning chocolate milk from her new dining-room carpet. Hordes of citizens had descended upon their home, driven by pure nosiness. Dr. Neely, who'd owned it before the Gardners, hadn't entertained many visitors, and rumors of its beauty had circulated for decades. Now the curiosity seekers were tromping through the rooms, peeking into medicine cabinets and inspecting closets.

"Quite a place you got here, Sam," Asa Peacock said.

"The quilt on your bed is especially nice," Jessie Peacock added. "Is it a family heirloom?"

A crash came from the general direction of the front parlor

just before Kyle Weathers sauntered around the corner and into the dining room. "Sorry about that, Sam, but you really shouldn't have lamp cords out where people can trip over them."

Back at the meetinghouse, Dale Hinshaw was exhorting the heavenly hosts to appear a bit more cheerful, though it was difficult to repeat "Glory to God in the highest, and on earth peace, good will toward men!" with a high degree of enthusiasm for two hours straight. Especially if you're the Hodges and had had a ferocious argument on your way to the meetinghouse to praise God and encourage good will toward men.

Sam spent the rest of the evening studiously avoiding his wife, who shot him dark glances when no one was likely to notice. He was dreading the time when the last person would leave and was giving serious thought to leaving with them, maybe heading off to a monastery for a time of spiritual renewal or some such worthwhile endeavor, until Barbara settled down and he could come home, sometime around Easter.

Though the goal of the progressive Nativity scene was to further the gospel, it was taking a fearsome toll on the marriages of its participants. Dr. Pierce and his newlywed wife, Deena Morrison, were engaged in a whispered debate about where they would spend their first Christmas.

"We spent Thanksgiving with your parents," Deena hissed. "Surely they'll understand us wanting to see my folks."

"I just worry about my mother. This could be her last year with us. She's not doing well."

"Your mother is sixty-six years old and will outlive us all," Deena said, leaving unspoken what she really thought of her mother-in-law—that witches don't die unless doused with water.

They'd pause from their argument to smile at the people walking past, then pick it up again when they fell out of earshot.

An occasional pilgrim, upon seeing Mary and Joseph, would inquire as to the whereabouts of the Christ child, and Deena would have to explain that it was a progressive Nativity scene and the Son of God could be viewed three blocks north at Harvey Muldock's home.

In early December, Sam had asked the elders to postpone the church's Christmas celebration until March, when things were less hectic and people needed a holiday to lift them over winter's hump and carry them into spring. It had gone over like a root canal.

"Why, I've never in all my life heard of such a thing," Fern Hampton had said. "Everybody knows Jesus was born on Christmas Day. It says right there in the Bible that they'd gone to Bethlehem for the holidays. You ought to read your Bible more, Sam."

Then he'd suggested a more contemplative Christmas program, perhaps some silent worship on Christmas Eve, maybe having Asa Peacock sing "Silent Night," then standing in a circle, lighting some candles, saying a prayer, and then going home to bed.

"I'd like to think that after everything the Lord has done for us, we could do a little more for Him," Dale Hinshaw had said, pausing for dramatic effect. "I believe the Lord is calling us to do a progressive Nativity scene."

And that's how Sam found himself sweeping up the pieces of the lamp Barbara had inherited from her grandmother. That the lamp was hideous and she'd been trying to dispose of it for several years mattered little; it was the principle of the thing—this pack of jackals slinking through her home, snooping through her rooms, spilling hot chocolate, and making a general mess of the place.

A minister's wife! How'd she get roped into that? It wasn't that she didn't love Sam; she cared for him deeply. She even thought highly of God. There were just days she wanted a secular life in which she didn't have to be on display as a model of Christian virtue.

That summer, her father had given Sam and her a bottle of wine, which they'd partaken of on their fifteenth anniversary. Opal Majors had rebuked her for placing the empty bottle in the recycling bin in front of their home. "You think this town wants to know about your drinking problem? Why can't you hide your nasty little habits like good Christians?" The day before, Barbara had gone to Kivett's to buy two wine glasses, and Fern Hampton had spied them in her shopping cart. "I hope those are for iced tea," she'd said.

Five years at the same church, and the honeymoon was over. No more hiding your bad side and putting your best foot forward. The vows had been made, the marriage consummated, and both parties had their eyes wide open. Sam and Barbara knew the church, the church knew them; annulling their union would take too much effort, so they worked it out. And every now and then, something wonderful happened; they saw one another in a new light and remembered why they had gotten together in the first place. But the night of the progressive Nativity scene was not that time.

Sam had a theory about Christmas and its toxic effect on marriages. In a word, gifts. This was the seventeenth year he and Barbara had exchanged presents, he was running out of ideas, and the strain was building. The year before he'd given her an exercise bike, something she hadn't asked for, which she thought implied a general lack of fitness.

"You think I'm fat, don't you?" she'd asked.

"Not at all. It's just that you can't do your walking when it's snowy outside, so I thought you'd enjoy having an exercise bike," he'd explained.

She'd accepted his explanation, just barely, but he knew the pressure was on to improve upon last year's performance.

Under the guise of visiting Shirley Finchum at the hospital in Cartersburg, he'd driven to the city the week before, to the north side where all the rich people lived, and had bought a dress she'd been eyeing in a catalog. The sales clerk had helped him select a matching bracelet, earrings, and shoes. It had set him back three hundred dollars, all his funeral money from that year.

Kyle Weathers had almost spoiled his surprise when he'd been poking around in the basement the night of the progressive Nativity and found the package hidden behind the furnace. He'd tromped upstairs, where he'd found Sam and Barbara in the kitchen. "Hey Sam, there's a package of some sort next to your furnace. I'd move that if I were you. Gets too hot, it might catch on fire, and up goes your whole house, kids and all."

Fortunately, the doorbell had rung just then and diverted Barbara's attention, so Sam ran downstairs and moved the sack behind some shelves in the old coal bins.

When the last of the crowd had left, he'd cleaned the kitchen, while she'd gone upstairs to put the boys to bed. He bided his time downstairs, hoping she'd fall asleep before he came to bed, but there she was, under the blankets, her bedside lamp on, reading.

She looked up from her book. "What was that package next to the furnace? Did you move it?"

"Just an old sack that had fallen down there," he explained, as he slipped into his pajamas and slid into bed. "Looks like it had been there for years. Probably when the Neely's lived here. I threw it away."

She thought momentarily of reviving their argument about his volunteering them for things without checking with her first, but decided against it. She didn't want to quash the meager bit of holiday spirit they had left. Besides, the chocolate milk hadn't stained their carpet and Kyle Weathers had done them a favor breaking the lamp, so she let it pass. She turned off her light, kissed Sam goodnight, snuggled in next to him, and promptly fell asleep.

Sam waited until she was snoring before rising from their bed and tiptoeing downstairs to the kitchen pantry, where, in search of carpet cleaner, he'd spied an unfamiliar box on the top shelf, behind the flower vases.

Sam had never been good at waiting until Christmas to see what he'd gotten and had been making regular sweeps of the house the past few weeks sniffing out his presents. Somehow, he'd missed this one. He scooted a kitchen chair across the floor, stood on it, pulled down the box—it was deliciously heavy—and opened it. An eighteen-volt cordless drill with a complete set of carbide-tipped drill bits. He was elated, thinking of the holes he could drill with it.

What a wife he had!

He repackaged the drill just as it had come, placed the box back on the shelf, arranging the flower vases in front of it, then crept upstairs to bed. He looked in on the boys. They were lying perfectly still in a sugar-induced coma, their mouths ringed with the remnants of hot chocolate. He bent and placed his face against his younger son's cheek until he stirred. "Love you, buddy," Sam whispered in his ear.

"Love you, Daddy."

Children, Sam thought contentedly to himself, are the berries.

Across town and three miles out into the country, Ellis Hodge was not feeling nearly so blessed. It had been a horrendous day and had not improved when he and Miriam had bickered all the way into town about whether or not to invite Ralph and Sandy to Christmas dinner. Now he was terribly unsettled and pacing around the house while Miriam and Amanda were asleep upstairs. Amanda hadn't smiled in a week; Miriam was similarly depressed. Even his livestock seemed more distant than usual.

This morning had been worse. In an effort to lighten the mood, he'd asked Amanda what she wanted for Christmas. She'd looked up from her blueberry pancakes, then asked him to give her the one thing he couldn't give. "I want you to love my father again. That's all I want. I want you to remember when you were little and he was your brother and you played with him in the hayloft and swam in the creek and shared a bedroom and stayed up late at night to talk. I want you to love him now like you loved him then. That's all I want. If you can't give me that, then I don't want anything."

Then she'd excused herself and gone upstairs.

Miriam had busied herself picking up the dirty dishes and carrying them over to the sink, while Ellis sat at the breakfast table stunned into silence.

"She just doesn't understand," he'd finally said. "I welcome him back into the family and everything is hunky-dory for a couple of months and she goes back to stay with them. Then the next thing you know he's drunk and slapping her around again and treating her like dirt. Can't she see I'm doing this for her? I don't like being this way. I would love to be on good terms with Ralph, I'd love to have my brother back, but it's not that simple."

Miriam didn't know what to say, so she hadn't said anything, which Ellis mistook for anger, which is why he'd spent the day in the barn and bickered with her all the way into town that evening.

Argument is unfamiliar terrain for them, and they don't traverse it well. They're at a distinct disadvantage compared to those couples who lose their tempers on a regular basis and have honed their reconciliation skills.

So Christmas Day passed quietly as an unspoken strain pervaded their home. Amanda received a new pair of blue jeans and a radio, which she politely thanked Ellis and Miriam for, then asked if she could go for a walk.

"Where to, honey?" Miriam asked.

"Oh, just around. I'll only be gone a few hours."

"All right then. Dress warm. It's cold outside."

She walked the three miles into town. An occasional car whizzed past. A mile out, she spied the water tower; then came the school and the meetinghouse and Kivett's Five and Dime. She walked through the town and out again, heading toward the tourist cabins where her parents lived. She paused in front of their door. A string of lights was taped around the inside of their window, flashing in a tired cadence. Ralph spied her through the window. He opened the door and drew Amanda to him, overwhelmed with pleasure.

"I've come home," Amanda whispered in his ear. "I've come home."

Eighteen

Another Christmas Day

Sam Gardner was picking up the Christmas wrapping scattered across the living-room floor. Ordinarily a safe undertaking, it was made perilous by the remote-control cars buzzing around his feet, zipping and zooming along the hardwood floor.

"Watch out," Levi cried, as Sam stepped toward a crumpled mound of gift wrap. Sam swung his foot wide to miss the car, lost his balance, and toppled onto the couch, shell-shocked.

Christmas was getting more dangerous by the year.

Barbara bustled in from the kitchen, the pleasant scent of roast turkey in her wake. "Sam, we don't have time for you to take a nap. Folks will be here any minute. Let's get cracking."

A family Christmas dinner had been Barbara's idea. Two weeks before, she'd convened a family meeting and laid out her platform. "We have this big house, and we just sit around on Christmas Day in our sweatpants, staring at one another and taking naps. Well, this year's going to be different. We're having your parents and Roger and Sabrina over and we're going to sit at the dining-room table in our nicest clothes and use a tablecloth and enjoy a nice meal."

Sam and the boys had been miserable ever since.

"Get off that couch, pick up this mess, and get your suit on," she barked at Sam.

"You there," she said, pointing to the boys. "Go take your showers, brush your teeth, and get dressed. Your father will help you tie your ties."

"Ties!" Addison shrieked, collapsing to the floor with a tragic flourish.

"Ties?" said Sam. "We have to wear ties?"

"Sam Gardner, I am trying my best to teach our sons good manners, and you're not helping."

"Come on, guys. Let's get dressed," Sam said without the slightest hint of enthusiasm.

He deposited the boys in the shower and began pulling on his suit. The year before, Harvey Muldock had given him a tie that showed dogs playing poker. He hadn't worn it yet, but now, in a passive-aggressive gesture, he pulled it from the tie rack, threaded it under his shirt collar, and fashioned a Windsor knot.

He hustled the boys through the bathroom, combed their hair, laid out their clothes, then clipped on their ties just as the doorbell rang. They marched down the stairs, the picture of gracious living, though thoroughly miserable.

His father, attired in his funeral suit, appeared as somber as his son and grandsons.

Sam's mother was wearing a strand of pearls that hadn't seen the light of day since Eisenhower was in office. She studied Sam, then licked her hand, and smoothed his cowlick. "Don't our men look handsome," she exulted. "Just look at them."

Barbara ushered them into the parlor, where they sat on chairs never intended to be sat on in the first place. They smiled awkwardly at one another, unaccustomed to this holiday finery.

Somewhere in the room, a stomach gurgled. "I've had the worst gas," Sam's father announced. "Started last night. Had some cheese balls over at the Muldocks' and been paying for it ever since."

Sam pondered how best to respond to his father's revelation. "Those cheese balls will do it every time," he said after a thoughtful silence.

Roger and Sabrina arrived a half hour later, dressed in their customary black.

It took twenty minutes to eat the meal Barbara had started cooking the day before. They pushed away from the table and reminisced about past holidays.

"What did Santa bring you this year?" Sam's father asked the boys.

They ran to their bedroom and returned with their remote-control cars.

"I hope those aren't battery powered," Sabrina said. "Did you know that in America we throw away enough batteries each year to fill the Empire State Building?"

"Now that's what I don't understand," Sam's father said. "How do they know that? You couldn't fill that building with batteries, 'cause every time you opened the doors to put more in, the ones in there'd roll right out and then you'd just have to start all over again. How do they know that?"

"Batteries aren't the worst of it," Sabrina went on, frowning like the earnest person she was. "It's packaging that's the real problem. All that cardboard to hold a little toy and people throw it away with no thought of recycling it. You recycle, don't you, Sam?"

"Religiously. Don't want to fill up the landfills."

Barbara stared at him, surprised by her husband's newfound commitment to the environment.

"Hey, Dad," Levi piped up, "remember last week when the trash man wouldn't take that old paint and you poured it down the storm drain?"

Sam smiled weakly, pushed a sliver of turkey fat around his plate, and tried to remember why he'd been so happy when his children had learned to talk.

Sam wasn't the only parent with problems that day. Across town, Ralph and Sandy Hodge were trying to explain to

Amanda why a tourist cabin wasn't a fitting place for a teenage girl to live.

"It isn't that we don't want you to be with us," Sandy explained. "You know we do. But you wouldn't have any privacy. There's not even room for another bed. We need a little more time to prepare a place for you, that's all. Then we can be together and it'll be so much nicer. Right now, we'd just be tripping over one another."

"Do Ellis and Miriam know you're here?" Ralph asked.

"I don't think so," Amanda said, wiping her nose with her shirtsleeve. "I told them I was going for a walk."

"We need to let them know you're here," Ralph said. "They're probably starting to worry about you. Why don't you call and tell them where you are?"

"First, I want to give you your Christmas present," Amanda said, pulling a small package from her coat pocket. It was a photograph of the three of them, taken at a picture booth in a mall during a rare period of sobriety for Ralph and Sandy. Amanda appeared to be around seven, and they were all dressed up. "Remember, it was Christmas Eve and you took me to the mall and bought me a doll." She'd kept the picture ever since, tucked between the pages of a diary she'd begun that same year.

The week before she'd bought a frame for the picture at Kivett's Five and Dime.

Ralph and Sandy looked at the picture, not saying a word, just swallowing hard and staring. After a while, Ralph cleared his throat and pulled Amanda to him, smoothing her hair with his hand. "That's the finest gift anyone ever gave us."

They all embraced, sitting on the edge of the bed, the only place to sit in the tiny room.

"We'll be getting a place real soon," Sandy whispered to Amanda. "Then we can be together like a family should."

They visited a while longer. Then Ralph wondered if Miriam and Ellis might be concerned about Amanda's whereabouts. "Probably ought to drive you back home," he said.

Back at Ellis and Miriam's, Ellis had phoned Asa and Jessie Peacock to see if Amanda had stopped to see them.

"Nope, we've not seen her," Asa reported. "You think someone kidnapped her?"

No, he hadn't thought that. Not at least until Asa had suggested the possibility. Now he could think of little else.

"She's been kidnapped," he wailed to Miriam. "Somebody's taken her. What's the number for the police?" He paused to catch his breath. "Or maybe she's run off with someone. Oh, Lord, did you have that talk with her yet?"

"No, not yet. I was going to, but the time never felt right."

"Well, thanks to you she'll come back here pregnant. You really let her down this time."

"Will you settle down! She's been gone less than two hours. She probably wants a little time to herself."

"Well, if you're not going to do anything, I guess I will," he declared. He pulled on his barn coat, climbed in his truck, and drove toward town, slowly, peering in the ditches in the event she'd been struck by a car and was at that very moment exhaling her last feeble breath.

He saw Ralph's car before they saw his truck and swerved across the road to block their path.

His no-good, drunken bum of a brother! He should have known. He flung himself out of his truck in a self-righteous fury, strode to Ralph's car, which had come to a stop, yanked his door open, and punched Ralph squarely on the nose. "Kidnap my daughter again, and the next time you'll get worse!" he said.

He'd never punched anyone on the nose, and it was hard to say which of the brothers was more surprised. But Ellis was the first to recover, and while Ralph sat staring at him and holding his nose, Ellis cuffed him again for good measure.

He then marched around the front of Ralph's car, seized Amanda by the right arm, pulled her from the car, and half carried her to his truck.

"He was bringing me home," she yelled. "Why'd you hit him? And, for your information, I'm not your daughter. I'm your niece. Now take me back to my dad."

That Ellis would not do. He threw his truck into gear and tromped on the gas, spinning his rear tires and peppering Ralph's car with gravel.

When they reached home, Amanda went straight to her room, refusing to talk. Ellis stalked back and forth across the living room, ranting about his brother in such coarse language

Miriam booted him out to the barn, then collapsed in her chair, her head spinning. What has happened to my nice, quiet husband? she wondered to herself. He's turned into a raving lunatic. She'd read in several magazines that raising children had a deleterious effect on certain people, but she'd had no idea.

As for Ralph, he was still seated in his car, his head tilted back, a handkerchief pressed to his nose to stanch the flow of blood. Getting punched in the nose, he was coming to realize, helped organize one's thoughts, and right now he was thinking how much his brother must despise him.

He entertained the notion of driving to his brother's farm and returning the favor, then decided against it. He and Sandy had been studying the Bible and that very morning had read about forgiveness, which had put him in a charitable frame of mind. He was grateful he hadn't just read about God slaying the Amalekites. Who knows how it would have ended? Instead, he drove back home to Sandy and their room at the tourist cabins, where she applied a cold washrag to his nose and consoled him.

"I guess this means we're not accepting Miriam's invitation to come over tonight for dinner," she said.

"Probably wouldn't be wise," Ralph sniffed. He picked up the picture of Amanda and studied it. "What a Christmas Day this has been," he said after a while. "I gain a daughter and lose a brother."

"We knew if we came back here, it wouldn't be easy," Sandy

pointed out. "And let's try to look on the bright side. At least he didn't kill you."

"There is that, I guess."

"How about some Dinty Moore beef stew?" she asked. "I think we have one more can."

"Sure, that'd be great. Getting beat up has a way of making a fella hungry."

She plucked the can of beef stew from the top shelf of their closet, opened it, and spooned it into their saucepan, which she set on top of the hot plate resting on their chest of drawers.

"How you feeling, honey?" she asked, while warming his meal.

"Better every minute."

"Maybe he didn't mean to hit you. Maybe he slipped and fell and hit you on accident," Sandy suggested.

"He hit me twice."

She winced. "I guess you can't call it an accident if he did it twice."

"Probably not."

A plume of steam rose from the saucepan. "Looks like your dinner is done."

She poured the beef stew from the pan into a bowl, then sat beside him on the bed and watched him while he ate.

"Nothin' better than Dinty Moore," he said.

"Someday we'll have a real house with a real kitchen, and I can cook you real meals."

"But I like Dinty Moore."

She laughed and snuggled in beside him. "One day, your brother will come to his senses and realize what a wonderful person you've become, and things'll work out."

"I hope that happens before he punches me in the nose again."

He finished his supper, washed the bowl in the bathroom sink, then sat in the chair beside the window, watching the sun set in the December sky as another Christmas Day slipped into memory.

"Dear Lord," he whispered, "forgive us all for all the hurt we cause."

Nineteen

Dale's Fine Form

It was the last Tuesday in January before Ned Kivett finally took down his Christmas display. He makes his money at Christmas and hates to see it come to an end. Santa's departure was duly noted by Bob Miles in that week's "Bobservation Post," and Owen Stout collected one dollar from every member of the Odd Fellows Lodge for correctly predicting when Ned would give Santa the boot and set up the window for Valentine's Day.

The lottery Kyle Weathers began in July to cash in on what appeared to be Dale Hinshaw's imminent demise had fallen by the wayside after Dale's stunning comeback.

Dale, now seated in Kyle's chair for his weekly neck shave, was pondering aloud why the Lord had spared him. "I can't help but think He wants me to give the Scripture eggs ministry another try."

Four years before, Dale's Scripture eggs ministry had come to a tragic end when his chickens had died of a poultry disease; he'd been lamenting their loss ever since.

Kyle, desperate to change the subject before Dale got wound up, turned to Asa Peacock. "How's life on the farm, Asa?"

"So far, so good," Asa reported. "Say, Dale, that sure was odd how your chickens died all at once like that. I never seen anything like that before."

"It's like the Lord Himself wanted it to end," Dale said glumly, still perplexed by this unfathomable evil even four years later.

Kyle unsnapped the apron from around Dale's neck and removed it with a hurried flourish. "There you go, Dale. All done. Next!"

Dale counted out the exact change into Kyle's hand, rubbed his hand across his reddened neck (this was the amazing thing about Dale Hinshaw—no matter the season, his neck was always red) and sauntered out the door.

It was an unusually balmy day for January, so he'd walked the three blocks to get his hair cut. On the way home, he stopped out front of Grant's Hardware to stand on the spot he'd collapsed the spring before. He'd been after Uly to place some type of plaque there memorializing the event, but Uly had resisted, even after Dale had pointed out that reminding people of the fragility of human life might bring them a little closer to the Lord.

Nora Nagle was helping her father, Clevis, change the sign at the Royal Theater. Dale paused to rebuke them for being in league with the godless liberals in Hollywood who were causing God Almighty to withdraw His protective hand over this once God-fearing nation.

"It's a Disney cartoon, Dale, about a fish," Nora said. "How is that perverting America?"

"I'll tell you right now, if you played that movie backwards, you'd see Satan worshipers. You mark my words!" he cried out, his voice rising to a fevered pitch.

Dale was feeling better than he had in months.

He stopped by the meetinghouse to see if Sam was there, but Sam had seem him coming and had slipped out the back door.

"Don't know when he'll be back," Frank the secretary told Dale. "But I'll be sure to tell him you stopped by."

"Tell him I caught a few mistakes in his sermon this past Sunday," Dale said.

"I'm sure he'll be delighted to hear from you."

"Maybe you should just have him call me."

"You got it, buddy," Frank said, as he eased Dale out the door.

It was almost noon, time for Brother Lester's radio program, so Dale hurried home. He'd written Brother Lester the month before inviting him to speak at the meetinghouse, but hadn't heard back. Brother Lester had mentioned the many requests he'd received, but that with one leg he could only do so much. Not only that, he'd been sequestered away doing research and was now poised to reveal a dark secret the Vatican had tried in vain to keep quiet.

Dale rushed along, positively gleeful at the prospect of this sordid revelation. Five minutes later, he was seated at the kitchen table next to Dolores, listening to Brother Lester labor for the Truth. What a blissful day it was turning out to be, full of opportunities to correct and reprove the wayward and lukewarm! Now to hear Brother Lester confirm what he'd always expected—that the pope himself was a member of the Masonic Lodge and had met regularly with Bill Clinton, a closet Mason, to plot a new world order—elevated his mood to mountainous heights.

"I knew it!" he said, slapping the table. "Didn't I tell you? Well, their secret's out now."

He thought of picketing the Masonic Lodge in Cartersburg that very evening and would have, except that he had a meeting of the church's Furnace Committee. Instead, he wrote a blistering editorial to the *Harmony Herald* and hand-delivered it to Bob Miles an hour later, demanding it be placed on the top half of the front page and not buried in small print in the classifieds, where Bob ordinarily ran his letters.

"You know, Dale, there are some people in this town who get tired of reading your letters. We can't run them every week," Bob pointed out.

"That's the problem with today's generation. They don't want the truth. They wanna have their ears tickled and keep going in their filthy sin and not be called to righteousness."

"Truth? You want to talk about truth? Do you really think God gave you a new heart so you could write nasty letters to people? Why don't you make yourself useful?"

Dale turned beet red and tried to speak, but could only sputter, he was so indignant. "Bob Miles, that's the . . . You'll not ever see me again . . . Why, I'll never buy your newspaper again." A harmless threat, since the newspaper was free.

He turned and stalked from the office, then spent the rest of the day preparing his devotional for the Furnace Committee meeting. He'd missed the last six meetings, what with his heart problems, and was concerned the committee had grown spiritually lax in his absence. It seemed to be a trend among certain townspeople. So he prepared a devotional explaining the history of the furnace in the Bible, recalling when three men of faith— Shadrach, Meshach, and Abednego—were tossed in the flames by the wretched Nebuchadnezzar.

"I tell you, if it hadn't been for the furnace, we wouldn't even have that story," he said at that night's meeting. "And what about in Matthew, chapter thirteen, when the Lord Himself said he'll send his angels to throw the evildoers in the furnace. Now how's He gonna do that unless we have furnaces?" He thought briefly of Bob Miles burning to a nice turn.

"I don't think Jesus really said that," Asa Peacock said.

"Yeah, I don't think God would do that to people," Harvey Muldock conjectured.

Dale shook his head in disgust. The committee's waywardness was worse than he'd feared.

But that battle would have to wait; he had more pressing matters to resolve, namely, the church's utter contempt for its Furnace Committee. That very month, the Budget Committee, headed up by Fern Hampton, who had been against the Furnace Committee from the very start, had decided not to give the committee its annual three hundred dollars for furnace maintenance.

Dale was fit to be tied. "These people have forgotten what it's like to be without a furnace. I say we shut down the furnace this Sunday morning and let 'em freeze their keesters off. That'll make 'em think twice about not giving us our money."

"We can't do that," Ellis Hodge said. "They'll just go home."

"Not if we lock 'em inside," Dale said. "The kids start losing their fingers and toes, and three hundred dollars for the Furnace Committee looks pretty cheap."

"What about you, Dale?" Asa asked. "You told me you had to stay warm on account of your heart transplant."

That doused Dale's fire considerably. Children losing their digits didn't faze him a bit, but his own discomfort was another matter entirely.

"I know what we could do," Dale suggested. "Let's all of us start designating our offerings to the Furnace Committee. Then we'd have all the money we need. Let me run some figures here. How much money do you give the church each week, Asa?"

Asa hesitated before telling Dale what he gave was a private matter.

"Yeah, I don't think it's anybody's business what someone else gives," Ellis Hodge added.

"Now that's where you're wrong," Dale said. "Acts, chapter five. Ananias and Sapphira didn't come clean and the Lord struck 'em dead."

"I don't think that really happened," Asa said.

"Yeah, Sam said someone probably wrote that to scare people into giving money to the church," Ellis Hodge said.

"That's the whole problem right there," Dale said. "We got ourselves a pastor who doesn't fear the Lord and the next thing you know they're cutting the funds to the Furnace Committee and the world's goin' to Hades in a handbasket and it's all Sam's fault. Boy, they stopped stoning people too soon, if you ask me."

This was Dale Hinshaw at peak form—singling out one person whose well-deserved death would solve all the world's ills. Unfortunately, people who apparently didn't love the Lord as much as Dale had made it nearly impossible to kill heretics, so he took another tack. "I hate to do this, but I'm afraid you all will have to step down from this committee. It's clear to me you're not spiritually qualified to serve."

Asa, Harvey, and Ellis looked at Dale, aghast.

"You can't do that," Ellis Hodge said. "You can't kick us off the committee. The Nominating Committee appointed us."

This was a technicality Dale was willing to overlook. "You serve on this committee at my pleasure, and I'm asking you to leave."

Harvey burst out laughing. "Dale, I think that operation made you loony. You're not the president of the United States. In fact, you're not even the clerk of the committee. Ellis is."

"I am?" Ellis asked.

"Yep. Remember, we take turns. Asa was clerk last year. You are this year. Next year it's my turn, and then Dale is clerk."

"Well, when it's my turn to be clerk, I'm going to throw off the whole lot of you," Dale screeched.

"You do that, Dale," Asa said. "We'll probably be ready to take a little break just about then."

With that matter settled, they played poker with matchsticks for two hours, then adjourned.

"Boy, it's a good thing I didn't die," Dale told his wife when he got home. "That whole committee has given themselves over to the devil. No tellin' what would have happened if I hadn't been there."

"I didn't think you'd be gone that long. I was starting to worry. How are you feeling?" Dolores asked him.

"I tell you what, this new heart is a champion. I don't know who it belonged to, but the Lord sure did bless him with a good ticker. I feel better than I've felt in years. Think I might even start up my Scripture eggs ministry again."

"Let's not overdo it, honey. You don't want to overextend yourself."

Cleaning up after the laying hens Dale had kept in their basement had soured Dolores on poultry evangelism, and she'd been vastly relieved when the Lord, in His inscrutable ways, had snuffed them out.

Dolores changed the subject. "You know, we haven't even met the donor family. I wish we knew who they were so we could thank them properly."

Despite his disappointment at not being able to fire the Furnace Committee, Dale was feeling magnanimous. "Why not let's call the hospital tomorrow and see if they can arrange a meeting? It might cheer them up to see what good use I'm making of my new heart."

"Let's do it," Dolores agreed.

"Say, Sam Gardner didn't call, did he?"

"Phone hasn't rang all evening."

"Huh. Frank said he'd have him call me. He must have forgotten. I'll call him."

"Honey, it's nearly eleven. He's probably in bed."

"Oh, he'll want to talk with me. It's about the sermon he gave on Sunday."

Dale dialed Sam's house.

"Hello," Sam answered rather groggily, after eight rings.

"Dale here. Just wanted to go over your sermon with you. Been a little concerned. Don't get me wrong, I think you need to talk about grace every now and again, but I'm concerned you're letting sinners off the hook. Thinking maybe it's time you preached on Romans 3:10."

"I'll keep that in mind, Dale. Thanks for your suggestion."

"'None is righteous, not one.' Can't go wrong with that verse," Dale said. "I tell you, Sam, if you only knew what sinners there were in this town, some of them right in our own church, you'd think twice about preaching on this grace stuff."

"I'm sure you're right, Dale. Can I go back to sleep now?"

"Not just yet. I've got a few more verses I want to share with you."

"Why don't you write them down and bring them by the office tomorrow. No, wait, don't do that. Just put them in the mail. I'll be looking forward to getting them, Dale. You take care now. Good night." And with that, Sam hung up the phone.

Dale brushed his teeth, put on his pajamas, and slid into bed next to Dolores.

What a day, he thought. He'd prophesied against the Nagles and their dalliance with Hollywood liberals, written an editorial against Bill Clinton and the Catholics, was on his way to restoring the Furnace Committee to its former glory, and had urged Sam to crack the whip on some sinners.

He pulled the blankets around himself, thanked God for his strong new heart, whose previous owner was obviously a God-fearing Christian, snuggled in next to Dolores, and then fell asleep dreaming of his Scripture eggs and the numerous heathens they would bring to the Lord.

Twenty

Secrets

*F*ebruary blew in with a snowstorm, twelve inches of
snow with gale winds, drifting shut the country roads,
snapping the power lines, and closing down the schools
in a dozen counties. Asa and Jessie Peacock had driven south to
Florida to visit his aunt and were stuck in the warmth and sun-
shine, trying to make the best of it. Asa had been glued to the
weather channel, watching a red radar blob park itself over Harmony. He'd phoned Sam, who'd mentioned they'd lost their elec-
trical power. "Miriam and Ellis lost power at their house too. You
may still have it out at your place, I don't know."

Asa fretted for an entire day before Jessie suggested he phone
their home.

"Why would I do that? There's no one there to talk to."

"If our answering machine picks up, you'll know we have electricity," she explained. "Then you can stop worrying."

He dialed their number and listened as their phone rang. Eight, nine, ten, eleven, he counted silently. "When does the machine pick up?" he yelled into the other room to Jessie.

"Sixth ring."

"Oh Lord," he cried out, pacing back and forth across his aunt's living room. "If we lost our power, then we lost our heat. Now the pipes'll bust and flood the place."

"Does that mean we'll have to buy new carpet?" Jessie asked.

"I suppose so."

"Good, I never have liked that carpet."

Back in Harmony, Dale Hinshaw was staring out his front window. "Just look at that sidewalk. Gonna be a sheet of ice if we don't get it cleaned off and salted."

"I told you I can do it," Dolores said.

"You think I'm gonna let a woman shovel my sidewalk? I'd never hear the end of it." He watched glumly as the snow fell. "Wonder why Sam hasn't stopped by to do it. These ministers nowadays sure aren't much for serving."

"Maybe if you treated him a little kinder, he'd have done it," Dolores snapped. Being cooped up with Dale for four days had taken a toll on her patience.

Their phone rang before Dale had a chance to take her down a peg or two with a Scripture verse. Dolores crossed the living room and answered the phone in the kitchen.

"Who is it?" Dale yelled from his perch by the window.

She held up her finger to shush him, which of course had no effect. "If that's Sam, tell him to get over here with some salt and get this walk cleaned up."

"We're looking forward to meeting you," Dolores said after a few minutes. "Next Tuesday then, at eleven o'clock, at our home. And why don't you plan on having lunch with us. Okay. We'll see you then. Bye-bye now."

Dale walked into kitchen as she hung up the phone. "He can't get here 'til next Tuesday? Heck, it'll all be melted by then. The elders are gonna hear about this."

"That wasn't Sam."

"Then who was it?"

"A Mrs. Betty Bartley."

"Humph, never heard of her," Dale said with a dismissive snort. "I suppose she wants to sell us something."

"Not exactly. She's the widow of the man who gave you his heart. She wants to meet you. So I invited her here next Tuesday."

"Oh, well. That's different." Dale rubbed the scar across his chest. "Be nice to meet her. I wonder where she lives."

"Up in the city. Her husband died in a car wreck. A woman in Ohio got his corneas, a man in Illinois got his liver, and you got his heart. A bunch of different people got his skin," Dolores said with a slight shiver. "Anyway, she wants to meet the recipients, and we're at the top of the list."

"How old was he?" Dale asked.

"Forty-two."

"What do you know about that! No wonder I feel so good."

Dale spent the rest of the afternoon at the kitchen table studying actuarial tables he had left over from when he'd sold life
insurance. "As near as I can figure," he announced just before supper, "with a forty-two-year-old heart—wait, was he a smoker?"

"I don't know. It didn't seem right to ask."

"He probably wasn't, or they would haven't taken his heart in
the first place." He scribbled a few more figures, then poked the
pencil point against the paper with a confident jab. "Looks like
I'll reach ninety-eight." He leaned back in his chair with a satis-
fied smile on his face. "You know what the Word says, 'The fear of
the Lord prolongs life, but the years of the wicked will be short.'"

"I wouldn't point that out to Mrs. Bartley if I were you,"
Dolores suggested. "She might not like you implying her husband was wicked."

"Wonder what he did to make the Lord so mad?"

"Maybe he didn't do anything to make the Lord mad. Maybe
he just had an accident."

"Not a sparrow falls to the ground that the Lord doesn't
know it," Dale intoned. "He must've really honked God off.
Whatever it was, I hope it isn't catching."

The next few days were warmer, the steely clouds lifted, and
by Friday the Hinshaws were stir-crazy and went to the Kroger
for groceries, passing by the meetinghouse on the way.

"Would you look at that," Dale said. "Sam didn't even shovel the church's sidewalk. What are we paying that man to do?"

"I thought the church had hired Uly Grant's boy to do that," Dolores said.

"No, I called him and told him not to do it, that we had a pastor who was perfectly able-bodied and there was no sense in paying someone else to do it."

He shook his head, mystified by Sam's indolence. "I just don't understand that man. We pay him twenty-five thousand dollars a year to work one hour a week, let him take a week off in the summer, give him a hundred dollars at Christmas, and he can't bring himself to shovel a little snow."

He pulled to a stop in front of the meetinghouse. "I got half a mind to clean it off myself. Maybe that'll shame him a little, watching an older man do his work."

Dolores thought of stopping him, but after a week of listening to him rant, the possibility of widowhood seemed pleasant. "I'll wait right here," she said.

He stormed from their car and marched into the meeting-house, past a startled Frank, into Sam's office. "I see the front walk's not been cleaned."

Sam looked up from his computer. "I wouldn't know. I use the back door. Billy Grant's supposed to shovel the front."

"Well, he was, but I told him not to, that we could do it ourselves."

"Thank you for volunteering, Dale. The shovel's in the front closet beside the water heater. You might want to put some salt down once you get it cleaned. Billy was going to bring salt pellets from the hardware store, but now that you've fired him, I suppose you'll have to get some."

Sam turned back to his computer.

"What about my heart?" Dale asked. "You want a man in my condition out there shoveling snow? I could die."

"Think how kindly the Lord would look upon you if you died while serving the Kingdom."

Dale hadn't thought of that. A snow-shoveling martyr for the Lord. He liked the ring of it.

"You're really going to let him shovel the walk?" Frank asked after Dale left the office.

"Best-case scenario, he shovels the walk so we don't have to. Worst-case scenario, he drops dead and I have to preach his funeral, but he won't be around to pester us anymore."

"I can see the Christmas spirit doesn't last long around this place," Frank said.

"First thing they teach you in seminary," Sam said. "Don't ever shovel the church sidewalk or mow the church yard, or you'll be stuck with it the rest of your pastorate."

"You want me to keep an eye on him, just in case?" Frank asked.

"Yeah, if he drops dead, drag him over to the Baptist church, so maybe their pastor will bury him."

"What's got you so on edge?"

Sam stood for a moment, looking out the window, a tired look crossing his face. "Oh, this Hodge thing. I guess Ellis punched Ralph on the nose on Christmas Day. Miriam is on the verge of booting him out to the barn to live. She wants to resign from the elders. Says she has too much on her plate."

"I always thought they got along real good," Frank said. "They seem close. Guess you never know about some folks. That's what I like about this job. You get all the poop on people."

"There is that," Sam said. "But I'd just as soon not know some things."

Outside, Dale was scooping the snow from the walk.

"Suppose we ought to help him?" Frank asked.

"Probably so," Sam said, walking over to the coat tree and pulling on his jacket.

With three of them working, it only took fifteen minutes. Then Sam walked the two blocks to Grant's Hardware, rehired Billy Grant, and purchased a bag of salt.

He finished broadcasting the salt just as the noon fire whistle sounded. He checked his watch, moved it forward two minutes, then stowed the shovels in the front closet.

"What's for lunch?" Frank asked.

"Doesn't much matter to me."

"How about the Legal Grounds? Today is grilled cheese day." And with that they were off.

Deena glanced up from the grill as they walked through the door. "Hi, Sam. Hey, Frank."

"Hi, Deena," they said in unison.

"A grilled cheese with tomato soup today," she said. "Or a tuna salad wrap with a fruit cup." They both grimaced.

"Grilled cheese with a Coke." Sam said.

"Same here, except for coffee," Frank added.

They sat at the table next to the window, to watch the passers-by. Across the room, Miss Rudy looked up from her book and smiled.

Frank rose to his feet. "Hello, Miss Rudy. How are you?"

"I am well, thank you, Franklin, and how are you?"

Frank blushed. "Just fine," he said, then sat back down.

"Franklin?" Sam said, stifling a laugh.

"Oh, hush up. You know it wouldn't hurt for you to treat me with a little more dignity."

"I'm sorry, Franklin, I wasn't aware you felt that way. I'll try harder, Franklin."

"So how's married life?" Sam asked Deena when she brought them their sandwiches.

Deena paused, blew a lock of hair from her forehead, and sighed. "When I see him, it's good, but I don't see him all that much. Today, for instance, he has the day off and is sitting at home while I'm here working."

"Maybe you need to close the place down," Sam suggested.

Underneath the table, Frank kicked Sam squarely on the shin. "He didn't mean that, Deena. Did you, Sam?"

Deena laughed and patted Frank on the shoulder. "I'd miss

Frank too much if I closed down." She smiled at Frank, causing his heart to flutter. There are few things more beautiful than a Deena Morrison smile. "You certainly have been a faithful customer lately. You and Miss Rudy. Don't know how I'd stay in business if it weren't for you two eating lunch here every day."

She pulled a rag from her apron pocket and swiped the table next to them. "Let me know if you need anything else," she said before walking away.

"You and Miss Rudy, eh?" Sam asked. "Down here every day, eh? Why, Franklin, you are full of surprises."

"Sam Gardner, has anyone ever told you that you have a big mouth?"

"Just my wife."

"Well, she's right," Frank said, then chomped into his sandwich, clearly agitated.

"Yes, sir, that's what I like about my job. You get all the poop on people," Sam said. "And just so you know, I give a wedding discount to senior citizens."

"The problem with you, Sam Gardner, is that you are ill-bred. Just because I stand up to greet someone doesn't mean I want to get married."

"Of course, it doesn't, and I apologize," Sam said. "Your love life is none of my business. I hope you'll forgive me."

"I ought to quit, take up golf, and leave you to take care of Dale Hinshaw all by yourself," Frank grumbled. "It would serve you right for all the trouble you've caused me. I was supposed to have a nice retirement, with lots of time to do what I wanted. Now I'm stuck with you, making peanuts, havin' to do all your scut work. What I was thinking?"

And so their lunch went, bickering back and forth, the customary wintertime conversation of most people in Harmony when the ravages of weather forced them indoors, where they irritated one another to no end, rubbing their edges raw.

Over at the Kroger, Dale and Dolores were squabbling over what to feed their visitor the next Tuesday. At the Hodge home, Miriam and Ellis ate their lunch in a gloomy silence. And back at the Legal Grounds, Deena looked wistfully out the window toward her home while Miss Rudy glanced up from her book, studying the line of Frank's jaw, how it ended in his thick thatch of unruly hair. Bachelor hair. There are secrets in this town that weigh heavily, like snow on winter roofs.

Twenty-One

A House Divided

T he snow left as quickly as it had come. A rare southern wind blew the clouds away, the sun made its first
appearance in a week, and by eleven o'clock the needle
on the large thermometer nailed to the side of Dale Hinshaw's
garage had swung clockwise to sixty-two degrees. Snow was
falling off the roofs in large, wet clumps, spilling down the necks
of unsuspecting persons as they left their homes for their Saturday
errands.

Ellis Hodge couldn't remember the last time the temperature
had varied so greatly in the space of a day, but had recalled reading something about it and spent several hours poring over past
issues of *The Farmer's Almanac* in intense research.

"Here it is. I knew it was in here somewhere," he said, reading aloud, even though Miriam and Amanda had gone for a walk and he was the only one at home. "Sioux City, Iowa, May 16, 1997. Thirty-three degrees in the morning, and ninety-one degrees that afternoon. I'll be darned. Just think of that."

He bent the corner of the page so he could show it to Miriam and Amanda when they returned, hoping it might ease the strain they'd been living under since he'd popped Ralph in the nose. Amanda had barely spoken to him since, and Miriam had been feeding him soup from a can.

Back in town, Bob Miles was seated at his desk in the *Herald* building. Inspired by the weather, he was pecking out an editorial about global warming. That'll bring the kooks out of the woodwork, he thought to himself. Bob has reached that liberating age when he no longer cares what others think of him.

Just the week before, Eunice Muldock had canceled Harvey's weekly advertisement. At her behest, Bob had attended the monthly meeting of the Red Hat Society, taken their picture, and pasted it on the front page of the paper underneath the headline *Old Bats in Red Hats*. Infuriating people, Bob had learned over the years, was the only way of ensuring he wasn't invited to attend every meeting in town. A year or two would pass, memories would fade, and he'd have to insult some people all over again.

He finished typing his editorial and placed it in the basket of articles to be included in the next edition, on top of a letter from

Dale Hinshaw, in which Dale, alarmed by Satan's inroads among the youth of Harmony, had urged "God-fearing Christians to march on the devil's camp and set the captives free!"

Like most of Dale's letters, it rambled. He began by taking a swing at Darwin, then took a poke at rap musicians and civil libertarians, suggesting some people had gotten a little carried away with the First Amendment and maybe it was time to crack down, maybe imprison a few people, lest Satan steal away more of their youth.

Bob reread the letter and sighed. What he wouldn't give for a thoughtful letter to the editor.

At that moment, Dale Hinshaw was seated at his kitchen table, pen in hand, drawing a sketch. "I tell you what, Dolores, this could be even bigger than the Scripture eggs. Here's what we do. We rent us a crane and haul it over to the football field at the high school and we get someone who loves the Lord and has a heart for young people and we heft them up in the air maybe fifty feet or so and then cut the rope and let 'em fall to the ground."

"And what would be the purpose of this?" Dolores asked.

"Shows the kids how Satan promises to lift you up, but lets you down every time. See, we paint the word *Satan* right on the crane and they see that and get the message."

"Who did you have in mind to drop to their death?"

"Oh, I don't know. Maybe somebody who was gettin' set to die anyway. Maybe Alice Stout. She's sorta slippin'. Might be doing her a favor."

"Don't you think her children would object?" Dolores asked.

"Now why would they do that? You think how much that nursing home is costing them. Besides, this way it's over with quick and she's eating at the heavenly banquet before we're even back to our cars."

"Why don't we think about this some more before we mention it to anybody," Dolores suggested.

Dale snorted. That was the problem with Christians nowadays: they were utterly lacking in conviction. Time was, Christians would have been happy to jump to their deaths, back in the olden days, when people loved the Lord.

He went to bed early that night, worn to a nub from worrying about Satan. He could scarcely wait until Tuesday. He lay still, the covers pulled up to his chin, thinking of Mrs. Betty Bartley and her husband's heart beating inside him. He thought of the crane and where he could rent it, then contemplated buying one and taking it on the road from school to school across the country, leading youth from their wayward path. He wondered if that was why the Lord had spared him. Then, for the briefest of moments, he wondered if maybe the Lord wanted him to fall from the crane. No, he didn't think so. He was a general in the Lord's army, after all, not a foot soldier.

He and Dolores skipped Sunday school the next morning. Sam had been leading a discussion on social issues, for crying out loud, blathering on about helping the poor and capital punishment and whatnot.

"What in the heydiddle does any of that have to do with Jesus?" he asked Dolores.

During worship, when Sam asked if there were any prayer concerns, Dale mentioned that the Lord might be leading him to a new work, but he wasn't sure. He was praying about it, and would others join him in prayer? Without waiting to see if they were willing, he launched into a prayer beseeching the Lord to do first one thing and then another, calling God's attention to things He no doubt would have missed, were Dale not around to point them out. "And Lord, we know that sometimes you call us to go the extra measure, maybe even ask some of us to give our lives for your sake. So if you're needing any of us to die here in the next couple of months, I just hope whoever it is will do it without complaining." He glanced over at Alice Stout, seated in the fourth row, her mind skipping in a groove like a broken record.

Maybe I'm being too subtle, he thought.

They spent the next two days cleaning their home in anticipation of Mrs. Bartley's arrival. True to her word, she pulled in their driveway at eleven o'clock. They watched as she alighted from a Volvo station wagon, a youngish-going-on-early-middle-aged woman, attractive in a competent sort of way.

"She's not wearing black," Dale observed. "Aren't widows supposed to wear black for a year?"

"I think they've changed the rules," Dolores said. "Just black to the funeral and that's all."

Their discussion was cut short by the sound of their doorbell. The Doxology reverberated throughout their small home. Dale sang along, as was his custom, while Dolores opened the door to greet Mrs. Bartley.

"Call me Betty," she said, shaking hands with Dolores, while glancing at Dale, who at that moment was praising Father, Son, and Holy Ghost.

"Dale Hinshaw here," he said, foregoing the "Amen" and thumping his chest with a flourish.

Dolores ushered them into the living room, where they sat across from one another.

"Care for a Scripture cookie?" Dale asked. "They're like fortune cookies, but they have the Word in them instead."

"Why, uh, yes, thank you," Betty Bartley said, reaching for a cookie.

"Tell us all about your husband," Dolores said. "I'm sure he was a wonderful man to want to donate his organs."

Betty Bartley's chin began to tremble. "He was wonderful. He was so . . ." She paused to compose herself. "So gentle, so kind. He cared so much about other people."

"What did he do?" Dale asked.

"He was an attorney. He worked for a law firm doing their pro bono work. Took all the cases no one else wanted. Mostly helping poor people."

"Funny you should say that," Dale said. "I never really cared for lawyer shows on TV, but ever since the transplant, I watch 'em all the time. Remember, Dolores, I was talking about that just the other day." He turned to Betty Bartley. "Do you like watching lawyer shows?"

"I don't watch much television," she admitted.

"I don't either," Dale hastened to add. "Just during the winter when I can't get outside. Mostly I watch Christian television. Have you seen Brother Lester's program? He's on the radio mainly, but every now and then he pops up on TV. We're trying to get him here to preach a revival at our church."

She thought for a moment. "I don't think I've seen him."

"You'd know it if you had. He's only got the one leg. Leans toward the right."

Don't all of them, Betty Bartley thought, starting to wonder if her husband's heart had been wasted.

"Tell us more about your husband," Dolores said. "What were his hobbies? Where was he from?"

"He grew up on a farm in southern Illinois."

"I grew up on a farm too," Dale said. "Then sold insurance."

"He liked to do woodworking," Betty Bartley added.

"So do I," Dale said. "I built that windmill in our front yard."

"Oh, and he loved this country." She leaned back in her chair, smiling at a pleasant memory. "He always talked about how blessed we were to live in America."

"No finer place," Dale said agreeably.

"He could recite the Declaration of Independence and the Bill of Rights from memory. Every Fourth of July, we'd have a party and he'd stand up on our picnic table and say them both by heart. He said they were the finest documents ever written."

Dale frowned slightly. "'Course the Bible's up there too."

"Oh, yes, he appreciated the Bible," Betty Bartley added. "He especially liked the book of Proverbs."

"And he belonged to a conversation club, he liked to fish, and he was a member of the American Civil Liberties Union. He was very passionate about our freedoms."

Dale blanched. A trickle of sweat erupted near his hairline and coursed down his forehead. He opened his mouth to speak, but for the first time in his life, words failed him.

Dolores, noting his condition, changed the subject. "How many children do you have?"

"We didn't have any children. We weren't able. But we have three nephews and two nieces, and he was very close to them."

"Aren't they the folks who sued to get prayer out of school?" Dale asked.

"My nieces and nephews? No, they're just children. They haven't sued anyone."

"No, the American Civil Liberties Union. They're the ones who won't let us put up the Ten Commandments?"

"That's not true. You can put the Ten Commandments any-where you wish, as long as it's not on public property. And you can even put them there, so long as they're part of a display with other historical documents," Betty Bartley explained.

Dale felt his heart begin to thump, then skip a beat. He

moaned, then fell back in his chair, nearly slumping to the floor. How could the Lord do this to him? After all he'd done for Him? Gave him the heart of a liberal! He wished he were dead.

"Dale, honey, are you all right?" Dolores asked, rising to her feet.

"The American Civil Liberties Union?" he croaked. "He belonged to the American Civil Liberties Union?"

"A card-carrying member for fifteen years," Betty Bartley said proudly. "Even served on the board of the state chapter. You've got the heart of a patriot beating inside you, Mr. Hinshaw."

This did little to ease Dale's distress.

Lunch was not the pleasant affair they'd anticipated. A ghastly pall had descended over Dale, and he ate half-heartedly, picking at his food. Dolores, in an effort to revive the conversation, asked Betty Bartley more questions about her husband and was rewarded with another sordid revelation: Mr. Bartley counted among his ancestors numerous Unitarians.

Dale pushed his plate aside. Sweat rolled down his face, now streaked a fevered red. "I don't feel so good. I think I'm gonna lay down."

"Is it your stomach?" Dolores asked.

"Something just north of there," he said glumly, rubbing his incision, which in the past hour had begun to itch something fierce.

Mrs. Betty Bartley excused herself to go visit a woman in Kokomo who'd gotten her husband's skin.

As Dale lay on the couch, the sun shone through their thinly woven draperies, causing speckled shadows across his face, giving him the appearance of being struck with a fearsome pox.

"Get Sam over here," he said, his voice weak and raspy. "I need him to pray for me before I cross over."

Dolores called Sam at home, who promised to be there as soon as he could. She sat beside Dale on the couch, smoothing back his hair and wiping his brow.

He appeared to be breathing his last, as if his body were at war, a house divided against itself, soon to fall. "Better hurry," he groaned. "I think they finally got me this time."

"Who got you, honey? What do you mean?"

"The liberals. They've been after me for years. Looks like they finally succeeded. Who'd have thought it? Let my guard down for one moment, and they slipped a liberal heart in me just knowing I'd reject it."

And with that, his body gave a great shudder, his eyes closed, and deep in his lungs a morbid rattle began to sound, like a viperous snake about to strike.

Twenty-Two

A Change of Heart

S am Gardner sat in the hospital waiting room slumped in
his chair, nearly asleep. He glanced at his watch, five
minutes before midnight, and was relieved to see an end
to what had been his most dreadful day in ministry. It had begun
innocently enough, with a quiet morning at the office following
by a pleasant lunch at home with his wife. Dolores Hinshaw's
phone call had changed everything.

It had taken him five minutes to reach the Hinshaws' home,
where he'd found Dale lying on the couch, clammy, listless, and
incoherent. He'd taken one look at Dale and calculated that by
the time Johnny Mackey arrived with his ambulance Dale might
well be dead. So he loaded the Hinshaws in his car and lit out for
the hospital in Cartersburg.

Dale revived within a few hours, cheered by the doctor's news that, even though his heart's previous owner had been a liberal, political perspectives were not contagious and Dale could expect to live the remainder of his life as hidebound as before.

"Thank the Lord," Dale said, his voice gaining strength by the moment.

Sam had driven them home at three o'clock, walking them to the door and promising to touch base with them the next day. He drove the three blocks to his house, pulled his car into the garage, and walked through the back door just as Barbara hung up the phone, visibly upset and near tears.

"That was Miriam. Amanda's been in a wreck. A dump truck driver ran a stop sign. They've lifelined her to the hospital in the city and need you up there just as quick as you can. She and Ellis are just now getting ready to leave."

"Call Frank and let him know," Sam said. "Have him get the chain of prayer going. But first call Miriam back. Tell her I'll be by to pick them up. They've got no business driving in their state of mind."

Miriam and Ellis were standing by the road next to their mail-box when Sam arrived. Miriam was pacing in circles, tears streaming down her face. Ellis was trying to console her and failing miserably. Sam helped them in the car, turned around in the driveway, and sped toward the city.

"Tell me what happened," he said.

"It's all my fault," Miriam said. She choked the words out,

barely able to speak for the spasms of grief coursing through her. "Ellis didn't want her to drive, but I told him we couldn't keep her at home forever. Now I've probably killed her."

"Don't talk like that," Ellis said, his voice trembling with distress. "This could have happened to anybody. The sheriff said it wasn't even her fault. The other driver ran the stop sign. There was nothing she could have done."

Then they fell silent, praying to themselves as the miles rolled away.

It took an hour and a half to reach the outskirts of the city, then another hour to make their way to the hospital through the rush-hour traffic. By the time they arrived, Miriam had collected herself, but Ellis had grown more distraught. Sam dropped them off at the emergency-room entrance, then went to park the car. He found a spot nearby and rushed into the hospital just as a nurse approached the Hodges.

"She's critical. They're still working on her. We don't know anything yet."

"We want to see her," Ellis demanded.

"Sir, right now your presence would be a distraction. Let's let the doctors do their job. Just as soon as it's possible, we'll let you in."

"Tell her we love her," Ellis said, his voice catching.

Sam steered them toward a group of empty chairs in the waiting room. "Let's sit down and pray," he said.

Sam Gardner had never been a proponent of public prayer, but that all changed as he sat beside Miriam and Ellis, clutching their hands. "Dear Lord, please be with Amanda. Guide the doctors and guard her life. Be with her and be with Miriam and Ellis, that they might know Your healing peace." He grew quiet, still holding their hands, praying a prayer that went beyond words.

There was a stir of motion near the door and they glanced up to see Amanda's parents, Ralph and Sandy, bustle into the room, their faces creased with worry.

"Where is she?" Ralph cried out. "Where's our girl? Frank called and told us she was here."

Miriam rose and went to them, taking their hands. "She's being worked on. They won't let us see her just yet."

She directed them to a set of chairs away from Ellis. No sense waving a red flag right in front of him. Sam walked over and sat with them for a few moments, consoling them.

Across the room, a mother and her daughter were airing their discord on national television as an audience cheered them on. What a sick world this can be, Sam thought glumly. He went over to the television and poked the power button off. They thumbed through the worn magazines for the next several hours, reading the same lines over and over, distracted with worry, before the emergency-room door opened with a bang and a doctor walked into the waiting room. "Hodge," he called out.

Miriam and Ellis and Ralph and Sandy stood.

The doctor looked at them, confused. "Amanda's parents can go see her," he said. "But just her parents. We don't want a lot of people back there. We're still working on her."

Ellis stepped forward, but Miriam pulled him back. "Honey, we're not her parents. That's Ralph and Sandy. Let them go be with her."

Ellis began to weep, standing in the center of the room, his body limp with misery.

Ralph placed his hand on Ellis's shoulder. "You go on ahead. You've been better parents to her than we ever were. Sandy and I, we can wait."

Miriam and Sandy stood watching their husbands. Ralph hung his head, the burden of his failures weighing especially heavy in this moment of confession. As for Ellis, he'd never been so thoroughly ashamed. The events of the past year ran through his head like a fast-forwarded movie—his cold rebuff of his brother, his hard words, his rigid refusal to believe anything good about his brother. My Lord, he thought, I hit my own brother, my own flesh and blood, and all he wanted was forgiveness. Ellis was glad his parents weren't alive to know the depths to which he had fallen.

The hateful weight that had burdened Ellis Hodge for years lifted from him and he turned to his little brother, crying, drawing Ralph toward him. "I'm sorry," he whispered. "Sorry I hit you. Sorry I was so mean to you."

Ralph held him, patting his back. "Don't you worry about any of that."

The two men stood, hugging one another, not speaking, just thumping one another on the back and healing their break.

"Why not both of you go in there and Sandy and I will wait out here," Miriam said after a bit. "It'll be good medicine for Amanda to see you two together."

"Let's go, brother. Let's go see your little girl," Ellis said, walking toward the door, his arm linked with Ralph's.

Sam watched on from his chair, dazed by this grace. Being a pastor at Harmony Friends Meeting didn't allow for many opportunities to witness reconciliation, and he stored the event away in his memory for a future sermon illustration. Of course, he'd have to change the names and wait until the Hodges died, but it bore remembering just the same.

They allowed Ralph and Ellis to stay for five minutes before shooing them out so Miriam and Sandy could see her. Amanda's head was swaddled in bandages, her lovely hair shorn off. An IV needle was taped to her arm. A nurse stood beside her, peering at the machines blinking by her bedside. Amanda's eyes were closed, her breathing shallow.

"We've got her pretty doped up," the nurse explained. "She needs rest. She took a real knock to the head. We're afraid her brain might swell, so we're keeping a close watch on her."

"How can you fix that?" Miriam asked.

"With drugs mostly. But if it gets bad, we might have to remove a portion of her skull," the nurse explained, taking Miriam by the hand. "I know it sounds terrible, but it isn't as bad as it sounds."

Miriam felt like vomiting and had to fight back a rise of bile.

"Is she going to make it?" Sandy asked, steeling herself for the answer.

"We're doing everything we can," the nurse promised. "It all depends on how her brain responds and whether she's bleeding internally. We're going to run a CAT scan in just a little while. We'll know a lot more after that. Now why don't you all go get something to eat, and if we need you, we can page you at the cafeteria."

So they went, all the Hodges and Sam, and pushed food around their plates for half an hour before trudging back upstairs to sit in the waiting room.

Around eight, Sam phoned home to hear his son's voices, thanking God they weren't lying in a hospital bed with holes in their heads. Barbara told him a group had gathered at the Hinshaws' home to pray. "It was Dale's idea. He said, and I quote, 'With folks in the meeting dropping like flies, we need to get right with the Lord before he takes us all out.'"

"Well, bless his heart," Sam said. "But shouldn't he be resting? He's had a long day too."

"The boys and I stopped past there and he looked fine to me. He was propped up on the couch, telling everyone else what to do. I guess the doctor did tell him he needed to stay off his feet a couple weeks. Besides, you know Dale. Having a cause perks him up."

Sam chuckled.

"Kind of makes you glad you gave him CPR, doesn't it?

"He does have his good side," Sam said. He paused for a moment. "You know, it feels weird saying it, but I'm actually growing fond of Dale. He's not all that bad a guy, really."

"He sure comes through in a pinch."

"That he does," Sam agreed.

"Miss you, honey."

"I miss you too," Sam said wistfully.

"When will you be home?"

"Just as soon as we know she'll be all right. But don't count on me tonight. Probably tomorrow morning some time. Can you call Frank and tell him I won't be at the office?"

"Will do. Be sure to tell the Hodges we're thinking of them."

He hung up, glad he could be present for the Hodges, but wishing he were home with his boys, ending the day with a game of checkers at their kitchen table. Wishing Amanda Hodge had driven through the intersection ten seconds later. Wishing, wishing, wishing.

The nurses brought them blankets, and they fashioned pallets across the chairs and settled in for a night of fitful sleep. They stirred around five the next morning and went immediately to Amanda's room, where the night nurse greeted them with mixed news. "She doesn't appear to be bleeding internally, but there's still swelling in her brain. We're trying a new drug to see if it helps."

They retreated to the cafeteria for breakfast, where Ellis and Ralph sat side by side revisiting the misdeeds of their youth in an effort to distract themselves.

"Say, Ralph, remember that time Dad went out of town on that big fishing trip with Abraham Peacock and told us to paint the barn?" Ellis mimicked their father's deep voice. "Now boys, I want you to paint the whole barn, from top to bottom, and I want it done by the time I get home."

"So we painted the windows too," Ralph said with a snort.

Miriam and Sandy had heard this story a hundred times, but laughed again, enjoying their husbands' camaraderie.

"How about that trip you and Dad and me took to Colorado?" Ellis said. "Remember that?"

"I never went on that one," Ralph corrected him. "That was just you and Dad. I asked to go, but Dad said no. Said someone had to stay home to finish the haying."

Ellis felt a pang of guilt.

"Can't tell you how many times I wished he'd have let me go. I started drinking that week. Oh well, water under the bridge."

"I'm sorry," Ellis said, reaching over to place his hand on Ralph's knee. The brothers sat quietly, each of them wishing they could undo certain decisions.

Sandy interrupted their musings. "Why not let's get some breakfast? I'm a little hungry."

"You do that," Sam said. "But I need to go home." He promised to return the next day. Then he remembered Ellis and Miriam were without a car. "How will you get home?"

"They can ride with us," Sandy said.

"Thank you, honey," Miriam said, reaching over to hug her sister-in-law.

"Well, then, I guess I'll be going. You all take care and I'll be in touch."

With most of the traffic heading into the city and Sam heading out, he reached the outskirts quickly, then turned onto the highway to Harmony. For a February day, it was pleasant, and feeling the sun on his face lifted his spirits. He found himself praying for Amanda one moment and the next moment thanking God for Ellis and Ralph's cease-fire. Who would have thought it?

Growing up in a small town, Sam could name family after family riven by discord. Brothers and sisters who went to the grave carrying their bitter animosities. People who went to church faithfully and taught Sunday school lessons about mercy and pardon and then would boycott the family Thanksgiving. So to see Ellis and Ralph make their peace was a balm to him.

He stopped past the meetinghouse before going home and told Frank all that had happened, then went home and kissed his wife, who made him shower and go to bed, where she lay down too, snuggling alongside him.

"Glad you're home."

"It's nice to be home," Sam said, staring at the ceiling. They talked about Ellis's change of heart, then about Amanda, and Barbara began to weep quietly, thinking of her.

Sam drew her closer and kissed her forehead. "She's gonna be all right. She's a fighter."

"Our sons are never driving," Barbara declared.

"It does make a person regret the invention of the automobile," Sam agreed. "We were probably better off riding horses."

Then Sam fell asleep, while Barbara watched him, feeling his breath rise and fall against her. She loved the smell of him. Soap, shaving cream, and the cheap shampoo they bought by the gallon from Kivett's Five and Dime that had a fruity smell and caused flies to dive-bomb their heads in the summertime.

After a half hour, she slipped out of bed to make lunch—grilled cheese sandwiches with tomato soup. Sam's favorite. Lunch for the conquering hero, her pastor, who moaned incessantly about his job, but deep down loved what he did. He would never admit to it, but after fifteen years of marriage, she knew. Could read him like a book.

After Sam awoke they ate lunch, then took the phone off the hook and went back upstairs to do what husbands and wives sometimes do when their children aren't home, especially when they've been reminded of the fragility of life—how vapor-like it is, here one moment and gone the next.

Twenty-Three

Love Is in the Air

manda Hodge remained in the hospital a little over a month—thirty-two days, nineteen hours, and six minutes, to be precise—according to Ellis Hodge, who spent much of that time beside her bed with Miriam and Ralph and Sandy. Asa Peacock fed Ellis's livestock, and Harmony Friends Meeting gave Miriam a vacation from serving as an elder, in hopes she wouldn't quit that post altogether.

Sam drove to the hospital twice a week, every Tuesday and Friday, to check on her progress. Although she'd sustained a serious head injury and no longer knew the words *polyribonucleotide* or *hermeneutics,* which she had once spelled to win the National Spelling Bee, she was still hands down smarter than anyone else in Harmony.

Her first week home, she slept on the couch, where Ellis and Miriam could keep a close eye on her. A steady stream of Harmonians stopped by to visit, including Bob Miles, who snapped her picture and ran it on the front page along with the story of her stunning recovery. Her classmates from high school gathered in the Hodges' front yard bearing a large sign wishing her well, accompanied by the school's show choir, who sang several songs to buoy her spirits and speed her recovery.

The Friendly Women's Circle took turns bringing in meals—a variety of casseroles, roasts, and homemade pies. Ellis gained ten pounds the first week they were home, and Miriam bumped up a dress size.

With Dale Hinshaw on bed rest and Miriam sidelined, the elders skipped two of their monthly meetings, and Sam was blessedly free to do what needed to be done without six people second-guessing him. He got more work done in two months than he had the previous five years. He changed the bulletin cover, fine-tuned the order of worship, cut out the children's sermon, and ordered new hymnals to replace the ones Moses had carried over from Egypt.

In late April, with Easter a scant two weeks away, he informed the congregation they wouldn't be holding their annual Easter pageant, that if they wanted all the hullabaloo they could worship at Pastor Jimmy's church that Sunday, where, in a reenactment of the Resurrection, Clevis Nagle would ascend to the heavens through the clever employment of pulleys and cables.

Not one person complained. They were tired too.

"Good call, Sam," Fern Hampton said while shaking his hand after worship. "We've had enough resurrections around this place. They're starting to wear me out."

"We're not doing anything special for Easter?" his wife asked on their walk home from church.

"Yes, of course, we're doing something special. We're going to gather with our friends and worship. You know, the old-time Quakers didn't go in for all these bells and whistles, and I think they might have had a point. Simplify, that's what I say."

"But what about the boys? Didn't you want to see them in the Easter pageant?"

Sam turned to his sons. "You boys want to dress up in flower costumes and be laughed at?"

"Not me," said Addison.

"Me neither," said Levi.

"That solves that," Sam declared. "Besides, I don't have time to head it up this year, which means it would have fallen to you."

"Why don't we simplify this year?" Barbara suggested.

"Sounds good."

And though Easter at Harmony Friends that year was simple, it was also beautiful, as a still lake surrounded by pine trees exudes a certain charm. God, in His infinite mercy, caused the organ to malfunction the week before Easter. Judy Iverson hauled her harp to the meetinghouse and when she began to play, everyone in the meeting room closed their eyes and dreamed they were in heaven. It was that good.

Consistent with the theme of resurrection, Amanda Hodge made her first appearance at church since her accident. When she walked in the door, people stood and clapped. It took the Hodges ten minutes to reach their pew for everyone wanting a hug. Ralph and Sandy and Ellis and Miriam walked beside her, beaming all the while, then took their seats in the Hodge pew, fourth one from the front, right-hand side, where the Hodges had planted their cabooses for five generations. Ellis reached his arm around Ralph and squeezed his shoulder. Ralph patted him on the knee. Amanda looked on, glowing.

There are certain times in church when a sermon is pointless, when words don't need to be spoken because the lesson has already been imparted. That Sunday was such a day. Sam opened his Bible, read the story of the Resurrection, and then had the good sense to sit down. The silence covered them like an old and comfortable blanket, draping in all the right places.

Dale Hinshaw stood and thanked everyone for their prayers. He was feeling much better, thank you. Then he sat down, just like that. No pontificating, no dire warnings that their souls were in jeopardy, no admonitions to straighten up and fly right.

Then Amanda stood and, reading from a list in her hand, expressed her gratitude for everyone who'd done anything for her—the ladies of the Circle for the food, Sam for visiting her in the hospital, Asa for feeding their livestock, Frank for organizing the chain of prayer, the Odd Fellows Lodge for their bouquet, her doctors and nurses at the hospital, and last, but certainly not least, God.

"Amen to that," Dale said from the seventh row.

They settled back into silence. Several minutes passed with the only sound the hollow tick of the Frieda Hampton Memorial Clock. Then a shoe scraped across the floor and the pew creaked as Ellis Hodge hauled himself to his feet, where he stood quietly for a moment before speaking.

"Sometimes we make our minds up about people and think we have them all figured out, then they go and do something and it changes our minds toward them. But then other times folks change and we don't believe it, and it causes a lot of hurt. And well, I guess what I want to say is that some people change, and we need to be grateful for that and reach out to them while we still can."

Miriam looked up at him, dabbing her eyes. Ralph bowed his head. Ellis reached down and placed his hand on Ralph's shoulder, then went on. "If any of you have anything against a family member or a friend, you need to forgive them or it'll eat you up inside."

His piece said, he sat down.

When they took the offering there were no bills less than a five in the plate. And when they stood to sing "Christ the Lord Has Risen Today," they sang so loudly, Judy Iverson and her harp couldn't be heard.

Just as Sam stepped up to the pulpit to give the closing prayer, Fern Hampton waddled out of her pew and made her way to the front of the meetinghouse. "Excuse me, Sam. I got an announcement to make." She turned toward the congregation. "As you may or may not know, today is Sam's fifth anniversary with us. Now I know there were some of you who didn't think he'd last that long, but here we are, still together. Well, anyway, the elders got together last week and we decided to have coffee and donuts after church today to celebrate Sam bein' with us. I hope you all can stay."

If there had a been a feather in the meetinghouse, it could have knocked Sam over.

Though most of them had hams in the oven back home, they stayed anyway, drinking coffee and eating donuts and shaking Sam's hand, thanking him for his service. They crowded around Dale, who told them of his narrow escape from liberalism. But the star of the day was Amanda, who received her admirers with such composure she reminded everyone of royalty.

"Isn't she something?" Ellis said to Ralph, looking on from the edge of the throng.

"You did a fine job, brother."

"I never did sell that mobile home," Ellis said. "It's still sitting in the field. Kept the electricity on to keep it heated, and we'd go over once a month or so to keep it dusted. Why don't you and Sandy move back in. Amanda's been talking about spending more time with you before she goes off to college. We can move her things over and you can be a family again."

Ralph didn't say anything. A tear leaked from his right eye, and he brushed it away. "A family," he said finally.

The next morning, Ellis drove his stock truck into town and moved Ralph and Sandy's belongings out to the farm. Then they hauled Amanda's clothes and bedroom furniture across the field and arranged them neatly in the back bedroom of the mobile home.

Sandy and Miriam cooked lunch in Sandy's new kitchen— an honest-to-goodness farm meal, not one thing from a can. Amanda looked on from the couch, dazed by her good fortune.

After lunch, Ellis sat beside her on the couch, smoothing her hair. "We love you like you're our own," he said. "You know that don't you."

"I love you too, Ellis."

"Come see us on Saturday mornings for blueberry pancakes, now, you hear."

"First thing in the morning," she promised.

They stood in the living room in a circle, everyone trying hard not to cry.

"Thank you," Sandy said very quietly. "Thank you for helping our family heal."

"We didn't do a thing," Miriam said. "You and Ralph are the brave ones. We're so proud of you."

Then Miriam and Ellis hugged them good-bye, climbed in their truck, drove a quarter mile down the road, and turned into their driveway. Ellis went out to his workshop in the barn and didn't come out the rest of the day, but when he emerged a little after six, his spirits were up. "What say we drive over to Cartersburg for supper tonight? My treat."

Their car was still in the shop, so they took Ellis' pickup. They drove through town, past the meetinghouse, and turned at the Dairy Queen to catch Cartersburg Road, passing the library and Miss Rudy's house.

It was a warm spring evening. The daffodils and tulips were in bloom around Miss Rudy's porch. That morning, Ernie Matthews had carried her porch furniture up from the basement, hung her swing in front of the window, and positioned her rocker alongside the small table where she set her iced tea glass of a summer evening.

Miss Rudy was sitting on the swing, with Frank the secretary seated beside her.

"Would you look at that," Ellis observed.

Miriam smiled and took his hand. "That's springtime for you," she said. "Love is in the air."

Ellis inhaled deeply and, even over the odor normally associated with a livestock truck, he could smell the pleasant aroma of sweet romance.

"It surely is," he said, taking her hand. "It surely is."

THE HARMONY COLLECTION

Don't miss master American storyteller Philip Gulley's other charming tales of small-town life.

PHILIP GULLEY's stories have become the *talk of the town!* A Quaker minister, writer, husband, and father, Gulley is also the bestselling author of *Front Porch Tales* and the acclaimed Harmony series. He and his wife, Joan, live in Indiana with their sons, Spencer and Sam.